THE BIKER'S BROTHER

Sons of Sanctuary MC
Book 2

Victoria Danann

Read more about this author and upcoming works at
VictoriaDanann.com

DESCRIPTION

- **Brand takes a job nobody wants in order to earn the respect of club members. Being third generation SSMC doesn't go very far in biker cred.**
- **Camden Carmichael is running from a psycho ex. Lucky for her that her father has the means to hire Sanctuary Security to protect her until the divorce is finalized.**
- **Two strangers set out on a road trip together. At the end of it, neither will ever be the same again.**

New York Times and USA Today bestselling author, Victoria Danann, adds a sizzling and surprising second book to the SSMC contemporary romance series.

Please note this book contains dark subject matter that may be unwelcome to sensitive readers.

Brandon St. Germaine was at the top of the billionaire playboy heap when he learned about a side of the family that had been kept secret. He left New York, moved to Texas, and took most of the corporate empire with him, restructuring so that he could spend time learning about the Texas motorcycle club branch of his family that had formed its own kind of dynasty.

His dad, president of the club his grandfather founded, spent three decades converting the club's income sources to legitimate business dealings. One of the biggest earners was the security service. When a ridiculously wealthy, but justifiably frightened father hired the SSMC to protect his daughter from the psycho she's divorcing, Brand got the job.

CHAPTER ONE

Texas

F OR ALMOST TWO years every hour that Brandon St. Germaine wasn't working at Germane Enterprises had been spent at the motorcycle club his grandfather had founded in 1975. He'd moved as much of the operation to Austin as possible and restructured his job description to free up time.

His father and brother had taught him about their side of the family and the legacy of the club. In exchange he offered suggestions here and there on how to make their own business enterprises more profitable. All in all he was satisfied with his new life, which was worlds away from the way he'd lived in New York. In fact there was only one thing he'd change if he could.

He wasn't a member of the club and couldn't be so long as he continued to run Germane. It was an odd situation, being part of the club's royal family and an outsider at the same time. Some of the members had become friends. Others regarded him with a polite distance that bore a marked resemblance to suspicion.

It was a Thursday in mid-October when Brandon

showed up at the clubhouse wearing jeans, boots, and a pink collared Polo. He knocked on the doorjamb of Brant's office.

Brant pulled his newspaper down far enough to see who was there. His eyes traveled down and back up before he said, "You look ridiculous. Men don't wear pink." He pulled his newspaper back up and continued reading as if Brandon wasn't there.

"This is faded salmon. Not pink. You know, Brash told me he expected you to get less grouchy after Mom moved in with you, but it's starting to look like that's not going to happen. Ever."

Brant moved his paper aside.

"I save my sweetness for where it belongs. Is there something you're wanting from me? 'Cause here you are on a weekday wearing 'faded salmon' instead of a suit."

"Yeah."

"Well? Spit it out."

"I can't join the club."

"First. Who asked you? Second. Why's that?"

Brand opened his mouth and closed it as he realized they'd never talked about it. He cleared his throat.

"I didn't mean to overstep or make assumptions. But if I was invited," he paused to gauge his dad's reaction to that, "I couldn't become a member because of my responsibility to Germane and especially to the health of Mom's interest."

Brant's nostrils flared slightly.

"I'll take care of your mother and you know it."

Brandon walked that back as fast as he could.

"Yes. Of course I know it. But she has a lot of personal history with the company. It wouldn't make her happy if it failed."

Brant put down the paper. After a few seconds, he nodded slightly.

"So that's what you wanted? To tell me why you're not joining a club you haven't been asked to join?"

"If you've always been this hard to talk to, I'm amazed that Brash turned out so good."

"I haven't had enough coffee for a critique of my parenting."

Brand shook his head.

"Okay. You're a bottom line kind of guy. Here it is. I can't become a member of the club. I understand the whole dues-paying prospect thing. And I'll never be able to do that. I guess the best I can hope for is hangaround. But I'd still like to have the respect of my family's... ah, associates."

Brant stood up. "Did you drive or ride?"

Brandon grinned. "Rode."

Brant suppressed a little smile of satisfaction.

"That's my boy. Let's go to Chuy's and have a little talk." He stretched and adjusted his package. "Lucky for you my manhood is secure enough to withstand being seen with a grown man wearing pussy pink."

Brand shook his head and followed his dad down the hall through the bar and out the door.

"You out, boss?" Ruby asked from behind the bar.

"Getting Mexican with my boy," he rumbled without looking over at her. "Whoever needs me, it can wait."

"Yes, sir," she said.

It was hard to say when it had happened, but gradually the position of bartender had acquired dual duties as admin. No doubt as the club grew its network of business enterprises, there was more to be accomplished than alcohol consumption.

The weather was close enough to heavenly to make Brant wish for days like that in the hereafter. As they sped toward Bee Caves he mulled over Brandon's place in their lives and came to some conclusions. He wasn't a follower. He was an innovator. And it was time to innovate.

They snagged a patio table next to the parking lot where they could keep a close eye on their bikes. They waved the menu away and ordered. Brant got the Elvis special as usual.

"And bring me a cold Lone Star, darlin'."

She smiled and nodded. "You pulling for Texans or Cowboys, Mr. Fornight?"

He grinned. "What do you think?"

She laughed. "I'm thinking Cowboys."

He shook his head. "I'm just going to let you wonder."

She laughed again. "You're no fun."

Brant gave her a smile that was still sexy as fuck at fifty.

"I assure you, darlin', I'm more fun than most people's hearts can stand."

Brand broke in. "He's married."

The waitress looked at Brand and giggled. "Yeah. Everybody knows that. What's your name?"

"Fornight."

She looked between the two of them. "Sure. I see that."

Brand got cheese enchiladas in red gravy and flautas in salsa verde.

"I'm going to be putting in extra time at the gym tonight." Brand smiled like he wasn't the least sorry. He slapped his abs. "Got to keep them tight if you want the ladies to fall to their knees when you walk by."

Brant looked at his son. "No self-respecting woman is going to give a second look to a dandy wearing 'faded salmon'."

Brand looked at his dad with renewed interest. "You homophobic or something?"

Brant pulled back. "Feared of queered? No!"

"I think you are," Brand challenged with a mischievous gleam.

"Then you'd be wrong. Now, unless you want to come out over lunch and tell me that you're wearing pink because you're a gay boy then let's change the subject."

Brandon laughed. "Whatever you say."

"You were making noises that you feel disrespected by the club."

"That is not the way I'd characterize what I said."

"You want to restate?" Brand thought about how else to put it, concluded that his dad's synopsis was more or less dead on, and shook his head. "So what do you want to do about it?"

"They're not going to accept me unless I participate in club revenue."

Brant smirked. "You want to make a donation to the treasury?"

"To use your phrase, don't be ridiculous. That would be more likely to cost me respect."

"Agree."

"Maybe I could work for the club. I don't have a lot of free time, but I can make some."

Brant took a swig from a cold long neck.

"Oddly enough, you and I are on the same track. I've got a job that no one wants to do. If you'd volunteer, it would go a long way towards making inroads. Maybe even waive prospecting."

"Waive prospecting? You can do that?"

"I can't do it on my own, but I can put it to a vote. I'm thinking most of the boys would trade a little principle to get out of this one."

"Why? What is it?"

"Security detail."

"Are you worried that I can't process more than two words at once?"

Brant cocked his head to the side.

"If you want to be in the club, you're going to have to learn some respect for the office of president."

"Okay. When I'm in the club, I will."

Brant couldn't help but smile. Brash had always been

a hell raiser. He came into the world so intense that he was wearing a little baby scowl between his eyebrows even in his toddler pictures. Brandon, on the other hand, was witty, easygoing, and, well, charming.

"So again, what's the job?"

Before Brant could answer, the food arrived.

"Always amazes me how fast they can get this shit ready to eat."

"Yeah. It's a miracle," Brand said. "Now stop dodging the question."

"Well, there's this girl." Brand sat back in his chair and started shaking his head. "Come on. You haven't even heard about it."

"I've heard the words security detail and girl paired with inside knowledge that everybody in the club is running from the job."

"Don't make up your mind without knowing all the facts. You wouldn't do that in business."

Brand knew his dad had a point. Using his dad's linguistic style, he said, "Alright. Lay it out."

"This girl comes from money. Like your mom. And you. She's from Boston. Anyway she got herself into a marriage with a bad guy and now her father's afraid for her life. The divorce is proceeding, but her dad wants to make sure she lives until the gavel comes down. I guess the ex is after her money and they have reason to believe he'll kill her if he can."

"Jesus."

"'Bout sums it up."

"How old is she?"

Brant searched his memory. "Twenty-four?"

"Wow, Father Time. Have you met the twenty-first century? If she's twenty-four she's a woman. Not a girl. And don't try to tell me that political correctness hasn't paid a visit to Austin. There are females all over the UT campus that would make Gloria Steinem look like Phyllis Schlafly."

"After what I just told you, what you want to focus on is whether or not I used the word woman or girl? It's too late to act out your teenage years."

Brandon picked up a flauta with his big hand and shoved half of it in his mouth.

"So you want me to go to Boston and follow her around?"

"No. I want you to transport her from New York to the compound. Here."

Brand narrowed his eyes at his dad.

"How dangerous is this? Really?"

"Fair to middlin'. I wouldn't be bringing it up if it weren't for the fact that I know you've spent the last year nosing all around our security company and going over the minutia of the way the veteran special forces' members handle jobs. I've seen the bruises you wear from all that martial arts training. And unless you've got a girlfriend who's beating on you, you work at it pretty steady. I know you're good with firearms because I've seen you at target play with your brother. Even when you're drunk, you hit your bullseyes. Last, you're smart."

That one made Brandon grin around a bite of enchilada. Brant ignored him and kept talking.

"So there are three things I'm looking at. First, you may be the most qualified guy we have. If I didn't think you could do it and get home safely, I wouldn't suggest it." Brandon was just about to say thank you when his dad added, "Your mother would string me up by the balls and then strangle me with my own entrails if anything happened to you."

"Nice image."

"Second, there's the respect thing. Doing that job would go a long way toward getting the respect you deserve from the crew. It's a big chunk of cash for the club and nobody wants the job. Third, like I said, this is important enough that I think we could get you a patch if that's what you want. You don't have to worry about working for the club. You already work for the club. By my reckoning, you made us $337,000 last year by consulting about the businesses.

"You found things we were doing wrong. Found things that could be better. Shut us down when we didn't have a prayer of going anywhere. Expanded when money was being left on the table."

"I'm kind of impressed that you pinpointed my contribution like that. I didn't know you're a data guy."

"Well. I am."

Brand took a swig of hard lemonade. "Did you already say yes to the job?"

Brant shrugged a big shoulder. "Too much green to

turn away even if I need to do it myself. Arnold said the dad could have taken out a contract for what he's paying us. And he's right. It's a *chunk* of change."

When Arnold had blurted that out in the meeting, he'd gotten several awkward minutes of silent stares from around the club table. They were bikers, but they weren't killers. Even back in the days when they operated outside the law, they hadn't been killers. At present they were businessmen who happened to like bikes and hold a certain disdain for authority and rules of all kinds.

"What's involved? Pick her up and fly her here?"

Brant laughed and shook his head. "If that was all there was to it, guys wouldn't be ducking around corners avoiding me. The man has hired the club to execute the disappearance of his daughter and keep her in the wind until after the divorce is final."

"Why does she need to disappear until after the divorce is finalized?"

"The soon-to-be ex-husband is dangerous and greedy. The girl's father thinks he may try to have her killed before the divorce goes through. He suspects this man of devising some clever means that would give him an airtight alibi while also making him eligible to inherit her trust fund."

"Who is it?"

"The client?"

"Yes."

"Severn Carmichael." Brand's eyebrows went up and he whistled. "I suspected you'd know who he is."

"Our enterprises have touched circuits now and then."

"He know who you are?"

"He probably knows who I am, just like I know who he is, but we've never met."

Brant seemed satisfied with that. "What do you think?"

"Let me make sure I've got this straight. I need to pick her up somewhere in New York, bring her to you, and make sure she's not seen or followed on the way."

"In a nutshell."

"What aren't you telling me? Why isn't it safer to shelter in place wherever she is?"

"He's scared. Really scared. Thinks this guy can get through any defense he can mount."

Brandon nodded thoughtfully. "When did you tell him we'd get her?"

"Day after tomorrow."

"Day after tomorrow? Forty-eight hours to come up with a plan and make arrangements to be away from the office?"

"Security will work with you on a plan. Taking time off work? Come on. You're the boss, aren't you? You want the job or not? If you do, I'll call a meeting and get a vote on patching you."

Brandon hadn't realized how badly he wanted that until it was offered. He'd thought it was something that would never be within his grasp, but suddenly there it was. He didn't really have a choice. Once in a lifetime offer to get the only thing he wanted that he didn't already have?

Hell, yes.

"Hell, yes."

Brant smiled as they stood up. He slapped Brandon on the shoulder and it made Brand's heart ache for the years he'd missed not having his father in his life.

"I'll call you later with the verdict," Brant said.

They mounted their rides and ignited the engines. The noise made all the patrons of Chuy's turn and look. The men wished they were on those bikes. The women wished they were sitting behind the men on those bikes.

Brant turned west on Bee Caves. Brandon saluted as he turned east.

BRANDON GOT A text at ten o'clock. He sat on the side of the bed and read it.

> **Brant:** *You're in. Be here tomorrow at eleven to go over the plan.*
>
> **Brand:** *Okay. I want to talk to the old man. Find out everything he knows.*
>
> **Brant:** *It's your call. Do not tell your mother about this.*

Brand laughed and set the phone down on the bedside table. He looked behind him at the woman sprawled on his bed wearing nothing but red thigh-highs. He slapped her derriere hard enough to make her jerk awake.

"What?" she said.

"Time to go," Brand answered.

"Go?" she said sleepily. "You're kicking me out?"

He stopped and stared at her. "Let me guess. You thought I picked you up at the Congress Club and it was true love."

"Well, no, but..."

He threw her clothes at her. "Get dressed. I'll call you a taxi."

"Asshole."

He looked at her like he was offended. "I'm going to *pay* for it."

Once he got Siri or Sherry or something like that out of his top floor condo, he turned on the TV, made himself a nightcap, and watched the stock market report. When he went to bed, he couldn't sleep. He felt a little like a kid who thought he was going to get the bike he wanted for Christmas.

AT ELEVEN SHARP Brandon rode through the compound gates and strode into the clubhouse.

"They're waiting for you in there."

Ruby was drying a glass. So she motioned toward the conference room with her head.

Brandon raised his chin at her while treating her to a drool-worthy smile. That was the only way Ruby could tell the difference between Brash and Brand. Brash had a sexy grin that he saved for Brigid. Brand had a drop dead gorgeous smile and he wasn't stingy with it.

Brant, Car Lot, Judge, and Miles were waiting. He nodded to all of them.

"Close the door," Brant said. "Let's get started."

AT ONE O'CLOCK the briefing was complete. Brandon had a good handle on the plan.

"Brand wants to talk to Carmichael," Brant told the group. To Brandon he said, "You have any objections to putting him on speakerphone?" Brandon shook his head. "Okay. Let me get him."

Brant grabbed the land line phone behind him and set it on the table. Putting on his glasses, he read the number from a little notebook he kept in his breast pocket.

"Mr. Carmichael's office," said a female voice.

"This is Sanctuary Security. Can you put him on the phone, please?"

"Just a moment."

The symphonic strings of the elevator music that everyone hates equally began to filter into the room over the speakerphone. The four men gave each other looks that said, "If he doesn't pick up in thirty seconds, I'm putting that shit out the nearest window."

"Mr. Fornight?"

"Yeah. It's me. Got the man here who's going to move your package. He wants to talk to you directly. That okay with you?"

"Of course."

"Mr. Carmichael, my name's Brandon Fornight." He glanced at Brant, who raised an eyebrow because Brand had always gone by St. Germaine. "Is there anything you want to add about this Trey Michaels? He was your son-in-law for three years. I'm sure you've got some personal insights that wouldn't turn up in a dossier."

"The main thing I want to get across, and I can't express this too strongly, do *not* underestimate this man. He managed to fool me and I'm not being overly vain when I say that's not easy to do. He doesn't seem to have a conscience and that, paired with almost unlimited resources, makes him dangerous as it gets. He's very likely connected to organized crime. If everything I've heard is true, his influence is," he broke off for a few seconds, "extensive."

"Okay," Brand said. "Just one more question. How does she feel about camping?"

There was a lengthy pause before Carmichael spoke. "My daughter camping. Under other circumstances I might be laughing until tears came to my eyes."

"I see," said Brand. "Is there anything else you want me to know?"

"Yes. If anything happens to my little girl, you are a dead man."

"Duly noted," Brandon said drily.

Brant spoke up. "I'll call you on the secure phone tomorrow morning with final plans."

"We'll be ready," said Carmichael.

When the call was ended, Brandon turned to Brant and said, "I didn't want to use the name St. Germaine because he'd probably recognize it and question why I, of all people, am escorting his daughter to safety."

Brant nodded. "Smart." He didn't add that it had given him a little rush to hear Brandon use the surname, Fornight.

CHAPTER TWO

New Jersey

BRANDON WAS PICKED up at Newark and taken to a warehouse where a van painted like a Con Ed truck was waiting inside. Camden Carmichael's luggage was also waiting. It had been shipped to a Fed Ex facility and held there until claimed by one of Brant's operatives.

"These her bags?" Without waiting for confirmation, Brandon unzipped and started going through her things.

"What are you looking for?" Dyson was a chocolate-colored guy with beautiful white teeth. The whites of his eyes were just as arresting, the color of arctic tundra. He'd picked Brand up at the airport in a beater, wearing jeans with holes, not the kind that looked like they'd been deliberately made for purposes of fashion. The kind that looked like the result of wear. The jeans complemented a long-sleeve tee showing bits of some message that had once, no doubt, been crisp and colorful.

Brand looked at the car, then looked Dyson over.

"No. Really. You didn't need to work so hard at trying to impress me."

Dyson was mildly amused. When they were both in

the car and pulling away, he glanced at Brandon and said, "We haven't been able to hide in a sea of dark suits and white shirts since the sixties. The only way we can stay inconspicuous is to look near-homeless. People don't ogle folks who are down and out."

Brandon nodded. "Makes sense."

Dyson eyed Brandon's search through the bags.

"Trackable devices."

"I checked already." Dyson sounded a tad indignant.

"Good. If we both check and find nothing, then we stand double the chance of being right."

Dyson seemed to relax with that explanation, hearing that it wasn't a commentary on his performance or a lack of belief in his competency.

"There's a room over there." He nodded toward a back corner. "It's got a bed, a TV, a refrigerator, micro-wave. We have you as go-time tomorrow at ten. You'll need to leave here at nine fifteen to be in position. Here's your cover."

He handed Brandon a black windbreaker with the Con Ed emblem on the left breast, where a pocket might be if there was one.

"Thanks." Brand took the jacket.

"Need anything else?"

Brand looked around. "Food in the fridge?"

"Yeah. More than you can eat."

"Then no. I'm good."

"Alrighty then. See you in the a.m."

BRANDON HAD JUST polished off two microwavable ham and cheese breakfast biscuits and downed eight ounces of orange juice when he heard one of the warehouse bay doors opening. He glanced at the clock on the microwave. Nine o'clock.

He slipped the Con Ed jacket on. Tucked his toiletries into his dopp kit, zipped the kit up inside his leather bag, and pulled the strap over his shoulder. He looked around the room one more time to be sure he hadn't left anything. It was force of habit. He'd left a Sig Heuer watch in a hotel room once. Needless to say, it didn't turn up in lost and found.

Sure. He could afford to buy the Sig Heuer company without even affecting his bank account, but even rich people don't like to waste money.

When he reached the Con Ed truck, Dyson was standing next to it. "Have a good night?" he asked cheerfully.

"I've had worse."

"No doubt. You need directions?"

Brandon let himself smirk since his back was turned putting his bag into the back next to the Carmichael girl's. He was as New York as it came and could have found his way around in his sleep.

"No. I studied up."

"You sure?"

"Positive, but thanks."

"Okay. The package is in play and on schedule. See you back here," Dyson looked at his watch, "before ten thirty."

Brandon nodded as he opened the van door and settled in behind the wheel.

WHEN CAMI CARMICHAEL left her building she spotted the three bodyguards her family had hired to make sure she was delivered safely into the hands of the SSMC. They were dressed randomly, one in a suit, one in jeans and a hoodie, one in athletic wear. One was across the street and two were on either side of the door to her building, spaced a few yards apart. Her gaze deliberately passed over them so that no one would notice that they drew her attention. She went inside the Starbucks that was on the street level of her Boston condo building.

When the barista handed over her cinnamon latte, she said, "Sophie. Can I please go out the back door? My ex is playing at being a stalker."

"Oh, sure. It's that way."

Sophie pointed, but Cami knew the way. She'd checked it out when she and her dad's people were devising her getaway. It was still dark outside, always helpful when you're running.

The car was waiting in the alley, just as had been planned. She climbed in the back, deciding that she didn't much like acting out thriller adventures.

"Good morning, Ms. Carmichael," the driver said.

"Morning."

"I'm Raleigh. Let me know if you need anything."

She looked out the window at the familiar sights of

her neighborhood and felt sad to be leaving it behind. *What I need is a normal life.*

When they reached the corner, they stopped long enough for the guy in the suit to get in.

When he closed the door, he said, "Nice to see you again, Ms. Carmichael."

She nodded and smiled, but her anxiety was probably evident. She didn't think she was cut out for clandestine operations.

"Hello, Logan."

Other than the large shoulder bag, she had no luggage. She and Logan went straight to security at Logan Airport. Normally she would have had them scan her boarding pass from her smart phone, but she'd been told to leave her phone behind.

She sat next to the window in the first row of first class and Logan took the aisle seat. The flight to LaGuardia was just a little over an hour. Just enough time for a Bloody Mary and two reruns of *Friends*.

When they gave the okay to deplane, Logan stepped into the aisle, which blocked other passengers from exiting before Cami. She hitched her bag up on her shoulder, walked up the jet way and turned toward baggage claim where a car would be waiting at passenger pickup. Halfway up the concourse she stopped at the Ladies room. Logan took up a post leaning against the wall, presumably waiting for the woman he was with.

Inside a handicapped stall, she removed her silk dress and pumps, donned jeans, a ribbed green hoodie, and high top Converse, stuffed her mahogany tresses under a black wig with a severe chin-length cut, and pulled a cream-colored knit hat over that. Her stylish slouch bag was reversible. She turned it inside out so that it was a muted satin stripe instead of burgundy leather. She threw the silk dress and pumps into the waste receptacle and exited the restroom, keeping pace with the fast-moving crowd. Logan didn't acknowledge her in any way.

A man wearing a black tee and dark slacks with a raspberry scarf had fallen in beside her. She wasn't alarmed. She'd been told to look for him. All part of the plan that seemed to be working.

So far.

As he escorted her to the exit he said, "My name's Loomis, Ms. Carmichael. I'll be accompanying you to the city. Keep your face down and turned toward me as much as you can."

She nodded as they got into the taxi line. She kept her face averted as he said until they reached their turn at the head of the taxi queue.

"The Park Lane," he told the driver.

The ride into Manhattan was silent. At least it was silent as soon as she figured out how to turn the volume off the commercial-playing video screen attached to the back of the front seat.

It was an overcast day, the perfect backdrop for a life that had taken a turn for the worse. When the taxi pulled up in front of the Park Lane on 59th, Loomis paid the driver and ushered her inside. He covered their reason for being there by getting a room while she went to the Ladies room off the lobby.

Inside she changed into a silk dress and pumps, and changed the black wig for one that was short auburn. Last, she put on sunglasses and the wide-brimmed black hat that had been rolled up in her bag. She kept the demure clutch, but left everything else inside the big slouch bag and stowed it all under the overhung sinks.

She headed out the Park Lane back door on 58th. The town car was waiting for her as planned, back door already open.

The man who closed her door got into the front passenger seat. He angled his body toward her as they pulled away from the hotel.

"Relax, Ms. Carmichael. Everything is going as planned."

"Alright," she said, feeling like the entire sequence of events was a surreal game, more like an out-of-the-body experience than anything. It was an odd, numb feeling and hard to describe. Like being part of reality physically, but not emotionally.

The back windows of the town car were so dark that people outside the car wouldn't be able to tell if there was a passenger, much less identify a person. So, if she'd been able to get to the car without being followed, she was probably safe. It was still rush hour. Again, that had been part of the plan. It's hard to be followed in rush hour traffic. Too many taxis playing chicken, squeezing into tight openings between cars.

"Would you like to listen to music, Ms. Carmichael?"

She pulled her attention away from the hypnotic fugue state of watching buildings go by and said, "Whatever you want."

Loomis turned to a satellite radio station that featured pop soft. She sighed and resumed watching the people crowding the sidewalks, busily going through the motions of heading to work, getting groceries, delivering documents, or whatever else top of the day meant to six million people.

Eventually the town car navigated stop and go until they reached the Park Right located adjacent to the Lincoln Tunnel. They pulled in next to a large sign that said Open Twenty Four Hours and drove to the service door where a van painted to match a Con Ed service vehicle waited.

Loomis opened the back doors of the van before opening the back door of the town car. He, the town car driver, and the Con Ed driver were all three out of their respective vehicles scanning the surroundings for any sign that they were being observed. Cami got out of the car and into the back of the van, where she sat on the rubber mat covering the floor. She was pretty sure it was covered in a millimeter of dust and grease in equal parts.

"Looks clear to me," Loomis told Brandon.

Brand nodded.

"Let your boss know we're on schedule and I've got it from here."

For a second she deliberated whether staying alive

was really worth the discomfort and humiliation of being jostled in the back of a dirty van like a used appliance on the way to the dump.

Brand took the tunnel under the river and drove to Newark without seeing his passenger or speaking a word to her. When he arrived back at the warehouse, he used the remote on the visor to open the bay door. Dyson was waiting, looking pleased that things were going according to plan.

Since Brand had left, they'd turned a section of the warehouse into a mini salon on call with bright lights on tripods, a chair with hydraulics, rolling stands and fancy sprayers attached to the sink.

He turned off the engine and got out. Dyson had already opened the van doors and helped the package out. That was the first time that Brand got a look at Cami. She'd pulled off her hat, sunglasses, and wig in the van. She looked over at him before she headed for the salon chair and his breath almost froze in his lungs.

She had the most unusual violet-colored eyes he'd ever seen and a heart-shaped face surrounded by long mahogany hair so glossy it looked like she was getting ready to do a TV commercial. Brandon knew that it would be a crime to do a radical make-over of a creature as perfect as Camden Carmichael. But it had to be done.

He moved her luggage into the green Chevy Tahoe they'd be taking for the first leg of their journey, then settled into a corner of the warehouse that was outfitted like a makeshift lounge with coffee, couches, and magazines. Repeatedly he tried to find interest in one of the articles, but his curiosity kept pulling his gaze over to the salon.

The stylist cut away a full twelve inches of dark shiny hair, then bleached the tips so that, instead of looking like a society babe, Cami looked more like a rock chick. A little tough. A little hip. And a lot of f.u.

The whole process took almost two hours. When it was over, her eyes were still arresting, but they looked different with smoky eye makeup and blond-tipped pixie hair.

Brandon had to give her credit. If she was attached to her former look, she didn't let on. She stoically walked to the restroom, put on a thin cotton tee, jeans torn at one knee, and a plain gray cotton hoodie. The pumps she'd worn into the warehouse were replaced with boots that could have functioned equally well for hiking or combat.

She thanked the stylist, walked to the van and climbed into the front seat. As Brandon slid in on the driver's side, she looked at him, really seeing him for the first time, and thought she saw something vaguely familiar. Deciding that she'd probably seen a model who resembled him on a store poster, she turned toward the front seeming resigned to whatever was coming next. She still hadn't spoken a word to Brand, nor he to her.

"You have a cell phone on you?" She shook her head. "Okay. Put your head down between your knees. I'll let you know when I'm sure we weren't followed."

She gave him a withering look, but complied, putting

her head down, presumably so that she wouldn't be seen while he pulled out of the bay doors on the other side of the building.

She was thinking this last humiliation was a bit of overkill because, post make-over, her own mother wouldn't recognize her. Not that her mother had looked at her closely for years.

She remained in that position for almost twenty minutes while they sped south on the interstate. After they turned onto Highway One, he said, "You can sit up."

He handed her a big thick U.S. atlas or, rather, plopped it in her lap.

"You're going to navigate."

"Just use GPS," she said.

He smirked. "This car is too old for GPS."

"Oh." She opened the atlas. She had a degree in art history. Surely she could figure out how to read a map. "I don't see why we can't fly."

"Because, if your husband is as resourceful as we hear, he could hack airport data bases for your name; even private airports keep information." He looked her over. "My name's Brandon, by the way."

"I know who you are," she said, looking out the window.

"Right. Have you decided who *you* want to be until this is over?" She looked at him blankly. "You need a different name. I'm not going to call you Camden..."

"Cami," she corrected softly, turning her attention to pulling at a thread hanging from the hem of her hoodie.

Brandon glanced at her, deciding that maybe he should reserve judgment before shoving her in the bitch cubby. Maybe the nice person had temporarily gone into hiding, a self-protective mechanism kind of thing.

"When this is all over, I'll be glad to call you Cami," he replied just as softly. "But for the next two weeks you're going to have to pretend to be somebody else."

After a slight hesitation, she nodded without looking up.

"Come on," he said. "When you were little, wasn't there some other name you wished your parents had given you?"

"Rose White." He thought he saw a ghost of a smile, but she didn't look up. "It's from a fairy tale. I really wanted to be the sister, Rose Red, but it didn't seem to fit."

"Rose White it is then. Most people aren't going to know it's from a fairy tale. They'll just think your first name is Rose and your last name is White."

"Okay."

"Nice to meet you, Rose," Brand said.

She turned toward him as if she was seeing him for the first time. Judging from the way she looked him over, she was. Her eyes lingered on the masculine angularity of his face, the offbeat haircut, the inked curls at the wrist and neck of his long teal blue tee that suggested a tat sleeve. She concluded that he was a working class, motorcycle-riding player with whom she had absolutely nothing in common. Except good manners. Possibly.

"Nice to meet you, Brandon."

He glanced down at the atlas.

"We're going to West Virginia." He pointed to a spot on the atlas that lay open across her lap. "Find us the most direct route by way of Harpers Ferry and keep us off the interstates."

"Off the interstates. Isn't that going to take a really long time?"

"It's not a race. It's the hide part of hide and seek."

She stared at his profile. "What exactly is the plan?"

"I'm taking you to our safe house in Austin. It'll be home until the judge has signed off on your proceeding. My job is to make sure you get there alive."

"Okay."

He turned on the radio and found a classic rock station.

"Just kill me now," she mumbled.

"What was that?"

She looked straight at him.

"The radio." She pretended to have to scream over the music. "You're not going to make me listen to that. Are you?"

He cocked his head as he stared at the road ahead.

"I'm nothing if not fair. What kind of music do you like?"

"Well, for starters, I like music that was recorded this century."

He took his eyes off the road just long enough to be sure she caught the glare he gave her.

"You want to do a passive aggressive dance around what you want? Or do you want to just tell me straight up?"

She pressed her lips together, narrowed her eyes, and decided she'd underestimated Brandon. She didn't think thugs had descriptions like 'passive aggressive' easily tripping off their tongues.

"Country," she said decidedly.

He gaped. "That is utterly impossible. A girl like you does not listen to country music."

She looked indignant.

"I certainly do. And what do you mean 'a girl like me'?"

He narrowed his eyes and glanced at her.

"Okay. If you really listen to country music then tell me one thing about Garth Brooks that only somebody who was a fan would know."

Without hesitating she said, "He actually wanted to be a rock star, but when he opened his mouth to sing, country came out instead of rock. So he gave into it and owned it. Although he did steal the showmanship the rock stars had perfected by then."

Brandon had no idea if that was true, but because she said it with so much authority, and because it wasn't the kind of thing a person would be likely to make up on the fly, he believed her.

"Alright. We'll take turns."

"Good. Me first."

He nodded just slightly. "Find your station."

She seemed to perk up at the small victory.

"How do you get satellite?"

Brandon smirked. "Seriously? How sheltered are you?" She frowned at the question and said nothing, since she had no idea how to answer. "This car is too old for satellite. You got radio. That's it. Make do."

She set to work turning the dial. He even got a little smile after she settled on a station. After all that work, before the first song was over, she was slumped against the passenger door, sound asleep.

He looked over at her sleeping form and shook his head. He could have changed the station but thought it might wake her and, for some reason, he didn't want to disturb her. So he was stuck with listening to twang and fiddle for what turned out to be hours. By the time she woke, he was beginning to tap his fingers on the steering wheel and was thinking country might not be all *that* bad.

CHAPTER THREE

West Virginia

WHEN SHE OPENED her eyes, she was looking out the passenger window at trees. The radio was forecasting heavy rain coming their way and stalling over the area for a couple of days.

She heard him say, "Good," under his breath.

She turned far enough to see the clock on the dashboard, briefly glancing at Brandon. She'd been asleep for hours. As she sat up straighter she realized she must have been out like a light because she'd slept through the discomfort of acquiring a crick in her neck.

"You're still listening to country?"

"Yes. But it's not the same station. We're too far away."

"Why didn't you change it to codger rock?"

"Codger rock? That's just mean," he scolded. "Can't pick up a station here. These hillbillies' mamas don't dance and their daddies don't rock and roll."

"Is that some obscure musical reference?"

"It's not obscure if you understand it."

She began trying to stretch out the kink in her neck

drawing Brandon's attention to the rolling of her shoulders. The way her shoulder blades moved inside the knit top she wore was, well, sexy. For that matter, the knit top looked soft to touch and was kind of sexy, too.

He almost slapped himself when he realized that his thoughts were headed south of the steering wheel. *Come on, Brand. It's a job. Not a pick up. Remember, it's just business.*

"We're close to White Sulphur Springs."

Her voice brought him back to the moment.

"You've been here before?"

"Yes. There's a private airfield right over there." Brand said nothing. "You wouldn't know this, but there's a grand resort close by. Perhaps the last truly great resort in the world. The Greenbrier." She sighed.

He smirked at the windshield. *'He wouldn't know this.'* Indeed.

His mother's family had taken one of the luxury "cottages" for Christmas every other year when he was growing up. They flew their company's jet to the private airfield she'd mentioned. He'd played golf in the annual Sam Snead Pro-Am every year of his adult life. Except for the last, when he'd been busy learning his way around Austin and a motorcycle club legacy.

"Where are we going?"

"Not the Greenbrier," he said, pretending reverse snobbery. "We have a reservation for the night at a little out-of-the-way cabin. After this, we'll stay where we find a vacancy if it's convenient and I think it's safe."

She eyed the camping equipment in the back of the SUV.

"I'm not especially big on camping."

"Really? I never would have guessed that."

"You making fun of me?"

He looked over at her. When her eyes got stormy, as they were then, the violet seemed to overtake the blue so much that they appeared almost purple. Exotic. To say the least.

"No. I'm not making fun of you. Liking camping or not liking camping isn't important in the grand scheme of things."

Slowly her lips spread into a smile. "The grand scheme of things?"

"You never heard the expression before?"

"Of course. I guess… I just didn't expect to hear it from you."

"Why's that?"

She was sorry she'd gone down that path because she didn't see a way out without being insulting. So she changed the subject.

"It's beautiful this time of year."

He smirked to let her know that she hadn't gotten the diversion past him.

"Yeah," was all he said.

HE PULLED INTO a roadside stop that had used frequently spaced short signs to advertise for the past five miles.

"I'll get food to go. You stay in the car."

She shook her head vigorously. "I can't stay in the car. I need to go to the bathroom."

"You can hold it until we get where we're going for the night."

"No, I cannot! What is the matter with you?"

He watched a spark fire behind her eyes that hadn't been there before, almost like it was spontaneously rekindling from ash.

"What's the matter with me? Didn't you go before we left New York?"

"Yes. I went before we left New York. But I don't have a bladder the size of a basketball. I'm a woman."

When he raised his hand to reach toward the passenger side visor, she flinched. And not just a little. He'd been planning to retrieve a burner phone he'd stashed there, but seeing her reaction, he jerked his hand back.

She pressed herself back into the seat looking like she hoped to melt into it and disappear.

He stared for a few beats before quietly saying, "I'm sorry if I startled you. I was reaching for something I left under the visor."

She was embarrassed to have jerked away from nothing. More than embarrassed. Humiliated. She hadn't always been a skittish little mouse. There'd been a time when she'd had enough confidence to roar like a tiger. After a couple of years with Trey, she cowered when a hired driver slash bodyguard tried to reach toward her side of the car.

She turned her head toward the window so that he

wouldn't see the single tear that escaped and ran down her face. She swiped at it like it was offensive.

"There's nothing to apologize for. It's my problem. Not yours."

BRANDON HAD TO give the girl credit. She was defiant in the face of something that had tried to break her. Since she was running from an ex, it didn't take a genius to figure out what it was that had tried to break her. The same person who had vowed to protect and care for her.

Without waiting for permission she opened the door on her side, got out, and started walking toward the entrance.

"Son of a bitch," he mumbled to himself as he scrambled out of the car, looking around the parking lot and up and down the highway. He had to jog to catch up to her just before her hand wrapped around the door pull. He grabbed her wrist and stopped her. "If you won't let me do my job, I will dump your ass on the side of the road and go home."

"You would not," she hissed.

"Try me," he shot back.

"What do you suggest then? That I urinate in the car?"

He pressed his lips together, eyes searching hers until he found what he was looking for. Truth.

"Come on. Stick to me like a shadow." He waited for her to respond. "I need a sign that you understand and agree."

With the height difference it was impossible to look him in the eyes without tilting her head back.

"Okay!"

She sounded as exasperated as a teenager being told she had to be home at midnight.

He stepped in closer to her, fully aware that it was an intimidation tactic. He hated doing that, since she'd already demonstrated being skittish, but her life might depend on them having an understanding.

"You're not going to give me a hard time. Your father has sworn to end my life if I fail to deliver you unharmed. So you *will* cooperate. Understand?" She nodded, but rolled her eyes in a rebellious, but feeble attempt at maintaining autonomy. He opened the door and guided her inside. "Restrooms?" he asked the cashier as they passed.

The woman didn't even look up. She just pointed toward the back.

He opened the door marked "WOMEN" and gently shoved her forward.

Fortunately it was a single room. One toilet. One sink. One trash can. No windows.

"Here you go," he said. "I'll be outside."

When he left, she locked the door and looked around. White tile on the floor and halfway up the walls. She liked white tile. It was easy to see if it was dirty. Not that it would have mattered. She needed to go badly enough that a lack of cleanliness wouldn't have been a deterrent.

Before leaving, she took a look in the mirror and almost gasped. She'd forgotten that she looked like somebody else. Somebody else with smudgy eye makeup made even more smudgy by sleeping against a vinyl seat for hours.

She wet a paper towel and tried to do a little damage control. She didn't think looking like a raccoon was a good way to lay low. Running a hand over her head, she wondered how long it would take to get used to looking like she was either homeless or well on the way to being homeless. She hadn't had short hair since she was a baby and it felt... strange. Maybe not more so than a road trip with a total stranger who didn't want to let her go to the bathroom.

Brandon had the sandwich shop make up a variety of sandwiches. He grabbed bags of chips, two apples, two bananas, a carton of orange juice, a dozen bottles of water, chocolate chip cookies and most of their supply of peanuts without ever taking his eye off the restroom door. He left one bag of peanuts just in case somebody came in who needed them like he did.

When she emerged, he caught her eye.

"Anything in particular you need for the night?" She shook her head. "You like chocolate chip cookies?"

She looked around at the convenience store offerings with mild disdain.

"Not if they're prepackaged."

"Oh. You're one of those."

"One of what?"

"One of those people who thinks that anything packaged is poison."

"Well. It is!"

"I have two apples, two bananas, orange juice, although technically that's packaged, and waters. I also have sandwiches, but those were wrapped up."

"Smart ass," she said.

He let it drop. She might have been born privileged, but she'd faced her share of hardship at the hands of some connected asshole who, according to Carmichael, might have some screws loose.

After leaving York they headed west. They'd spent most of the day on two lane black top. The past few hours had been hilly and meandering. The best part was that they couldn't be followed without him knowing it.

Brand handed her the printed directions to the cabin to read out loud. It was starting to get dark and the cabin was secluded.

The keys were right where the owner said they'd be. Under the second large rock from the first step to the porch.

The cabin was cute. Unpaved driveway. Wooded on two sides and backed up to a running stream. A little rustic dollhouse. Two tiny bedrooms, with a shared bath in the small hallway between them. The beds were covered in colorful quilts that were very likely made and purchased locally. It wasn't the Greenbrier, but at least it wasn't camping.

Brandon checked out the house then immediately pulled all the shades down.

After looking around, Cami turned on the TV. Without missing a beat Brandon walked over and turned it off.

"Hey," she said.

"No TV," he said unceremoniously.

"Why not?"

"I need it quiet so I can hear what's going on around us."

She thought about arguing, but decided against it. After all, he was trying to take care of her. There were a few hardcover books amongst knickknacks. She picked up one bound in red with gold lettering. It was a biography of the Count de Sade, the contemporary descendant of the Marquis for whom sadism was named. She claimed the big armchair and opened the book, doing her best to ignore Brandon.

After careful consideration of the options, Brandon set Cami's luggage down in the living room. When she heard crashing about a few seconds later, she found ignoring him impossible. She got up to go see what was going on.

Brandon had moved the large antique armoire in front of the bedroom's two windows.

"What are you doing?"

He didn't look up. "Blocking the windows."

"Why?"

He didn't reply. After placing the chest where he wanted it, he moved on to the back bedroom. He threw pillows and bedding on the floor before pulling the mattress off the bed.

"What are you doing now?"

"Pulling this mattress out into the hallway so I don't have to sleep on the floor."

"Why would you sleep on the floor? There are two perfectly good beds in this…" she looked around, "doll house. At least there were before you disassembled one of them."

"I'm going to sleep here in the hallway tonight where I can keep an eye on you."

"That is ridiculous," she said.

"You're entitled to your opinion, but it doesn't count for much. That's how it is." After putting the mattress in place, he threw the quilt and pillows on top of it.

"Why did you say 'good' about the rain?"

"What?" He looked confused.

"In the car. The radio said rain is coming and I heard you say, 'Good'."

He took in a deep breath and willed himself calm.

"Everything has two sides. It makes travel slower, but it also makes it difficult to either find or follow you." She didn't seem to have anything else to say on the matter. "Sandwiches in the kitchen." He smiled. "Along with a few non-packaged items. It will be a few days before tofu will be readily available again."

She sniffed as he turned away. When she thought he wasn't watching, she took her time leisurely appreciating the way his broad shoulders tapered to his waist like the shape of the letter V. The way his muscles rippled under the Henley he wore was fascinating enough that she wanted to ask him to repeat certain movements.

The fact was inescapable, especially when he seemed to take up most of the space in a tiny little house. He was an extremely hot guy. But Cami wasn't a one night stand kind of woman. Even if she was, she suspected he regarded her as all business. Like he said, she was a box of widgets. Besides that, she couldn't imagine having anything in common with Brandon.

She'd been raised with money, gone to the best schools, and had even been to an Inaugural Ball. What could she have to talk about with a bodyguard from Texas? She knew practically nothing about him, but what she did know she didn't like.

He'd covered himself with tattoos. At least part of himself. He was okay with eating poison food like he was immortal, and had awful taste in music. Worse, he was imperious in the most heavy-handed and distasteful way possible.

She ate a turkey sandwich in the kitchen while reading her book. When she was ready for bed, she opened one of her bags and rifled through it. She took her toiletries and her night clothes into the little bathroom to change and emerged twenty minutes later wearing Gucci tartan pajama bottoms and a hoodie.

"It's freezing in here."

Brand looked up from doing whatever he was doing with his assortment of firearms that he'd carefully laid out on the coffee table. He appeared to have been oblivious to the temperature. He spotted the thermostat on the wall by the hallway.

After fiddling with it for a couple minutes, he said, "Nothing."

"It's not working?!?"

"That's what 'nothing' means. It's not going to be that cold tonight. Bundle up."

She made a show of exasperation, stomped over to her bags, and proceeded to put on a sweater, a knit hat, and a pair of thick socks while intermittently glaring at Brandon like it was his fault.

He smirked. "Overreact much? It's September!"

"I don't care if it's July. I'm cold!"

"Okay."

He shrugged and went back to what he was doing, appearing to have lost interest in the drama.

After she was outfitted for sleeping outdoors in the Arctic, she sank down on the mattress, pulled the quilt around her and, to her surprise, went to sleep.

The sounds of furniture moving woke her some time later. She opened the bedroom door.

"What's going on now?"

"Nothing," Brand said. "Go back to sleep."

He was moving the coffee table armory so that it was easily accessible. When he was satisfied with where it sat, he switched off the lamp, laid down, and pulled the quilt over his body.

"Are you done?" she said.

When he didn't reply, she closed the door a little too hard, for punctuation, and settled into bed again.

The next time she woke it was to the sound of raindrops on the roof. She lay awake for several minutes listening to the rain and feeling remarkably safe with the armoire in front of the windows and Brandon situated just on the other side of the door. She pulled the quilt under her chin, sighed, and was asleep before she could examine that thought too closely.

The next time she woke it was because a pillow had been thrown at her head.

With as much outrage as she could muster when she was drowsy, she said, "What the fuck?"

"Get up. We're going. You've got five minutes to get in the car."

She looked around. "It's dark."

"Exactly."

"I need to take a shower."

"You smell fine."

"First, how would you know? And, second, that's not the point!"

"Four minutes."

She pulled herself up, went to the bathroom, and brushed a hand over her hair.

When she came out, he said, "One minute."

Without changing clothes, she pushed her feet into her boots and said, "Fine. How's this?" She stood there in her tartan pajama bottoms, combat boots, multiple sweaters and knit hat.

"Not for me to say. This is not a fashion show," he responded drily.

She pursed her lips. "You got an umbrella?"

"You won't melt."

"Ugh! What is wrong with you?"

Brandon stopped for a second, thinking that maybe his attitude did need some adjusting.

"Just concentrating on vigilance is all. I'm not trying to make your life suck. I'm trying to make sure you have a life. After this is over, whether or not it sucks will be largely up to you."

He walked into the kitchen, banged through the cabinets until he found the large garbage bags and brought one to her.

Understanding the gesture as a kindness, she took the black plastic square gratefully and began unfolding it.

"I'll be back for you when I've got the bags in the car."

"Okay."

Two minutes later Brandon instructed Cami to lock the cottage front door while he kept watch. When she returned the key to its hiding spot, he ushered her to the car as fast as possible without worrying about cover from the rain for himself.

When he slid into the driver's seat and started the car, she said, "You're drenched."

Without looking at her, he said, "In a few minutes, when the engine's warm, I'll aim some warm air my direction."

She shook her head. "That's not going to dry you off. How are you going to protect me if you get the flu? You're not invincible you know."

"Getting wet doesn't give you the flu," he said as he pulled out onto the road. "It might make me a little uncomfortable, but it doesn't make my immune system more vulnerable. Influenza is caused by a virus. Rain clouds don't carry viruses. People do."

"Well, thank you for the lesson, science guy," she said sarcastically.

"You really thought that getting wet makes you sick? Do you also think the Sun circles the Earth?" His brief grin was a little charming even if it was seated in ridicule.

She narrowed her eyes. "I'll put my education up against yours any day."

Brandon grew serious as he studied the pattern the headlights made on the dark road ahead.

"You might not want to do that. You don't know much about me."

"So you're saying you're that famed but elusive poet slash philosopher who chooses to work as a longshoreman because he believes we're intended to work with brain, body, and spirit?"

He glanced over at her face dimly reflected in the dashboard lights and screwed up his face.

"What!?!"

She slumped down in the seat and sighed.

"Well, that proved nothing. If you were him, that's exactly what his reaction would be."

"You're a strange girl, Rose."

"I'm a woman, Brandon."

"Whatever you say."

"I'm not the only person in the world who thinks females in their mid-twenties are past being 'girls'."

"Are you trying to start a fight?"

She thought about that for a minute. "Maybe."

"Why?"

She thought about that for another minute.

"Maybe I think it's safe to fight with you."

"Safe?"

When she didn't say more, Brand concluded that it had been a while since she'd felt like she could safely voice an opposing view. She was exercising the privilege. Taking it out for a run. With him.

"You want to talk about what happened?"

"Happened?"

"With him?"

She glanced at the clock and shook her head.

"Not at five freaking twenty in the morning."

He shrugged. "Up to you. It's my turn to pick the music." He reached for the radio.

"It's a long story."

"Well, since we're going to be stuck in a crate together for days, it's a way to pass the time." He smiled at her. "Who knows? You might give me a reason to be enthusiastic about guarding your body."

"That pillow you threw at me this morning felt like you're already pretty enthusiastic."

Without another word he began scanning the radio signal. With his left hand on the wheel he went up and down the range of stations before settling on a mix of rock old and new. When the first song ended, the DJ announced that the system was going to be sitting on top of a forty thousand square mile area including parts of West Virginia, Kentucky, and Tennessee. She warned drivers to be safe in a voice far too sexy to sound alarming, but the message was received nonetheless. It was raining where they were and it was going to be raining where they were going, too.

Brand began happily drumming his thumbs on the steering wheel when the DJ's admonition was replaced with a song by *Stink Fist*.

After a few seconds, Cami reached over and turned off the radio.

"Okay. You win. No more torture. I'll talk."

"*Stink Fist* isn't torture," he said. "Wait until you hear *Sick Puppies*."

She stared. "That's not a real band."

"Yeah." He nodded. "It really is."

"There should be a law."

"You're stalling. Give me something else to listen to. If *Stink Fist* is off the table, you're up."

"Why do you want to hear this?"

"What else have we got to do? You've got a story that I've become a part of even if that was by contract. So I'm curious. How did a…" he smiled, "well-educated *woman* such as yourself end up here in the rain in a car too old for satellite sounds or navigation, leaving West Virginia in the dark? With me."

"Is this in confidence?"

"Are you asking for it to be?"

She bit her lip. "Yes."

He waggled his head back and forth.

"Sure. I'm not very big on carrying gossip anyway."

"Hmmm. I took you for a tongue wagger."

"Stalling."

"Alright. Alright." She faced forward, like she didn't want to know his reactions. "I met Trey at a party, a fund raiser for Catholic Charities. I'm not Catholic, but you know… Boston." She said that as if the name of the city carried a world of background information and explanation. "It's good for the family business."

Brandon knew a lot about attending charity events and giving generously because it was good for the family business, but he wasn't about to share that they had that in common.

"Somebody I'd known from school was there and introduced me. Mary Donovan," she added, like the name was somehow pertinent. "I'd noticed him staring at me throughout the evening. It would have been impossible not to notice because he's not the sort of personality who's easily overlooked. Well… and he's very good-looking."

Brandon shifted his weight in the seat when he heard that. It bothered him that she thought the villain she was running from was good-looking, though he had no idea why. Why should he care what she thought about her ex's looks? He reached for a bag of peanuts and ripped it open with his teeth.

"He immediately launched a full courtship press. Apparently he decided on sight that I was going to be the lucky girl."

"Woman."

"What?"

"No double standards. If I can't call you a girl, you can't call yourself a girl."

"Oh. Right. It's just an expression."

When she didn't resume her story, Brand prompted her. "It's just an expression when I say it, too. Go on."

"Ah, well, this is harder than I thought. I've never told the whole story before."

He glanced over at her. "Not to anybody?"

"Nope. Not even my mother." She laughed. "Of course she's the last person who'd be interested."

"Your dad is interested. I know that for a fact."

She nodded. "I don't know how I would have been able to pull away without his help." She sighed. "So he did that thing that predators do. Now I know how to recognize it because I've done a little research, but at the time, it just looked like a very attractive and successful guy was head over heels in love with me and desperate for my attention.

"It was nonstop flower deliveries and handwritten love notes. He even showed up at work to take me to lunch two or three times a week."

"Work?"

"Yeah. Work. I'm, well, I guess I should say I *was* a junior Art of the Americas curator at the MFA." He whistled and gave her a look that made her feel defensive. "I know what you're thinking. That I got the job because of my family. And you're right. I did. But it's not like I didn't do the work. I have an M.A. on the subject. I spent a year of high school in Mexico City and two years at the art museum in Sao Paulo."

Brandon raised an eyebrow.

"You speak Spanish *and* Portuguese?"

She smiled. "Well, that's a surprise."

"What is?"

"Most Americans think Brazilians speak Spanish." Brandon shrugged. "Yes. I speak Spanish and Portuguese. And a little bit of French."

"Combien coûte un peu?"

"Well, Sir Bodyguard. I'm even more surprised."

"Work takes me all over."

She nodded.

"To answer the question, I know enough that I could get around a French menu without using an app."

"So you were saying he would take you to lunch."

She seemed to deflate a little. Like the conversation had turned halfway pleasant and that tenuous grip on cheer was jerked out from under her.

She faced toward the windshield.

"It was flattering. *Really* flattering. I think maybe there's something deep in the core of femininity that longs to be pursued like that. For all appearances, he made me believe that I was desired above all other women, that not only did he only have eyes for me, but that he would always feel that way. And I mean, what woman could resist that?"

Brandon's only response was a deep sigh.

"I guess you're thinking that I was really naïve. And gullible," she said.

"I wasn't thinking that. My thoughts were more along the lines of thinking this guy is growing in douchebagness with every new syllable you speak."

"You know, you don't talk like a bodyguard."

"You keep saying that. How many bodyguards have you had?"

"Um. You're the first? Okay. So point taken. Maybe I'm not in a position to claim authority on how bodyguards talk in general. I just *suspect* they don't talk like you."

The rain was coming down so hard that Brand was forced to slow to twenty miles an hour. He couldn't see farther than the projection of the SUV's headlights.

"You get easily distracted. You know that?" he asked.

"I'll have you know I'm quite capable of concentration."

"Well?"

"So where was I?"

Brandon rolled his eyes.

"You know exactly where you were." She reached up to run a hand over her head and gasped. "What's wrong?"

"Ah, nothing. I'm just not used to not having any hair."

He glanced over at her.

"It's different from what you're used to, but it still looks good."

She looked at him with surprise, not expecting a compliment. "Thank you."

"You're welcome. Music or story. Your choice."

"You're kind of confusing. You say something nice and dovetail that with blackmail."

"You're stalling, Rose."

"Okay. Okay." She unzipped her jacket and aimed the warm air vent away from her body. "I told you he was good-looking. And successful. Well, add charming and sophisticated to that." Brandon felt the muscles in his throat tighten. "The reason I'm telling you all this is so you won't think I was crazy to fall for somebody like him. He pushed every button. Metaphorically speaking."

"Why do you care if I think you're crazy?"

"I don't," she said a little too quickly and a little too defensively. "Never mind. It was one of those whirlwind romances you hear about. At least that's what I thought it was.

"Three weeks after I met Trey, we were having dinner with my family to announce the engagement and show off my obscenely showy diamond. He didn't ask me what kind of ring I wanted. Now I recognize that as an early warning sign, like foreshadowing in books. You know? But at the time I thought it was kind of romantic that he wanted to surprise me with the ring *he* wanted."

"Hold on. I may be off on this, but don't a lot of guys just go out and buy rings?"

"Maybe they used to. These days, I'm pretty sure most consult with the bride-to-be about what she wants to wear twenty-four seven for the rest of her life."

Brandon nodded. "When you put it that way…"

"Anyhow. My family was more than okay with it. Especially my mother. And, well, why not? He looked good on paper." She let out a bitter little laugh. "He looked good in person. Gave every appearance of being the catch of the century. So they gave us their blessings and my mother spent the next nine months planning a society event to remember. I don't know how much it cost, but my dress alone was nutty expensive. The wedding was at St. Paul's Cathedral. We're Episcopal."

She looked at Brandon for a reaction, but there was none. She studied his handsome face reflected in the dashboard lights for a second before continuing.

"One thing about St. Paul's. We got our money out of the train on that dress because it's like a mile down that aisle. Every little girl's dream. We had the reception at the Copley because the club wasn't nearly big enough for Mom's guest list." She made a derisive sound. "She couldn't even get everybody into St. Paul's. So some people were invited just to the reception." She slumped down further into her seat and leaned back, looking out at the dark rainy night. "What a waste."

She suddenly turned her whole body in the seat so that she was partially facing Brandon.

"After we got back from our honeymoon my maid of honor told me that Trey had propositioned one of my bridesmaids at the reception. Tried to get her to say yes to a clandestine quickie.

"I've always wondered what I would have done if I'd found out on the spot that night. Would I have thrown the whole thing over or would I have given him a chance to explain it away and let the whole thing play out? I don't know."

CHAPTER FOUR

Kentucky

S HE TURNED BACK toward the passenger window. "I need coffee."

"First place we come to, we'll stop."

"Promise?"

Brandon smiled.

"Yeah. I could use a jolt of Joe, too. Maybe a donut."

"You can't be serious."

"About donuts? I'm deadly serious about donuts. I could do a whole Bubba Gump list on fried bread and the wondrous things that can be done with it. There's only one thing in the universe more amazing than donuts and that's peanuts."

"How do you keep from turning into massive love handles?"

"You been checking me out, Rose?"

She couldn't read his expression very well in the dim light, but his tone sounded teasing.

"I can tell the difference between you and the clerk at the Stop and Go if that's what you mean."

He laughed.

She was funny.

That was unexpected.

"Sit ups."

"What about them?"

"I do sit ups. I run on a treadmill. I eat stuff I want, but I don't eat *everything* I want."

"Hey. Was that the Kentucky border sign? Why?"

"Why what?"

"Why do you go to so much trouble? Usually guys who watch what they eat and work out like that, well, they're either gay or candidates for magazine covers. Sometimes both."

"You got me. I have been on magazine covers."

She barked out a laugh, having no idea that he was being serious.

"Yeah. Me, too."

"You do sit ups?"

"I'd rather give donuts a wide berth."

Brand shrugged.

"To each her own. At this rate I don't know how long until coffee."

They were still creeping along. The rain wasn't letting up at all. The windshield wipers waved back and forth at top speed, but their rhythmic beating did little to improve visibility. He got out another bag of peanuts.

"Wow. You're really addicted to those."

"Maybe. I think if I couldn't get any I might be willing to kill."

They'd only passed one car since leaving the cabin. If

there was a bright spot in the predicament, it was, as Brandon had said, that it would be impossible to locate Cami in that storm.

"Is that a light?" she asked.

"Yes, it is."

They pulled under the overhang of a gas pump island and the pounding rain immediately sounded further away. The combination fuel and convenience store was a welcome sight.

"Stay in the car while I get gas. I'll pull the car up to the door afterward and get coffee." He smiled. "And donuts."

Before she could reply he was out of the car letting cold air in. It was still early fall, but the rain had cooled everything down and made it unseasonably chilly. With the heater turned off, the car became instantly cold and she needed coffee even more. She reached for the garbage bag under her feet.

When Brandon got back into the car, his eyes went to the garbage bag she was holding.

"You don't need to get out. I'll get what you want."

"Bathroom."

The way she pressed her lips together when she said that one word told him that it was a fight he was going to lose.

"We haven't been on the road that long." He launched a weak protest knowing it was pointless.

"I'm getting out."

He huffed, but started the car and pulled up to the

store. It was brightly lit and he could see a clerk inside. Otherwise, they were the only people around.

As soon as he stopped the car, she was out and running toward the entrance. He followed and, again, was drenched within seconds. Not that he'd ever gotten completely dry from the last soaking.

"Whew!" The clerk smiled as they dashed inside. "That rain! It's coming down!" He offered a smile and a nod.

Brandon nodded in return.

"Restrooms?"

"That way." The clerk pointed to the back.

Brand guided Cami to the rear and, as before, looked inside to be sure there was no threat. He gestured for her to go ahead.

When she came out five minutes later, he was leaning against the wall opposite the doorway with his arms crossed. Her eyes flicked to the way that pose made his biceps bulge before returning to his face. At the same time his eyes ran the length of her tartan flannel pajama bottoms and back to the knit hat she'd pulled over her head just before exiting the car. She knew she looked like a grunge holdover street person and suddenly felt self-conscious about it.

Without a word, Brandon straightened and walked toward the coffee. She followed like she'd been ordered to fall in.

She pulled one of the biggest cups from the stack.

"I'll have a venti," she quipped as she set the cup under the dispenser that said 'big, bold flavor'. "If you want, I can drive for a while."

Brandon hadn't anticipated the offer.

That was unexpected.

"Maybe later. If the rain lets up."

"That's why you should let me drive now. Too much tension. We should do a rotation thing. Two hours on. Two hours off."

That plan was a lot more appealing than he wanted to let on.

"Even if I was considering that, I've only been driving for an hour." She shrugged and took a sip of her coffee after putting a full inch of cream on the top. "I'm surprised you're okay with dairy. Doesn't take much provocation to get health nuts to start ranting about milk."

"I don't consider myself to be a health *nut*. Just a reasonably knowledgeable and prudent person."

Brand barked out a laugh.

"Whatever. Let's see what kind of donuts they have."

She scoffed, but caught the mischievous glint in his eyes. He was teasing her. Wasn't there some rule about bodyguards getting too familiar with clients? On the other hand, she had opened the door for that. He was surprisingly clever. When he wasn't making sure the stick up his ass was firmly in place, he was passable company, too.

There were aisles of poison disguised as food. Close to the register there were two apples and three bananas.

She took one of the apples, one of the bananas, and pulled two waters and a cranberry juice out of the case for later.

Brandon glanced at the stash she laid on the counter.

"That's it?" he asked. "It's a long time until lunch."

She looked over her shoulder at the yards of candy, jerky, crackers, cookies, chips, and... "Wait a minute." She pulled six packages of cashews off the holder then grabbed a pack of hand towels from the auto mainte-nance section and brought them back to the register.

"Good," he said. "A growing gi... woman needs pro-tein." He lifted an eyebrow. "And her towels, I guess."

She smiled, finding it sort of endearing that he'd made an effort to refrain from calling her a girl.

They stood at the door for a second, both dreading the dash to the car in the beating rain. He looked down at her.

"On three." She nodded and brought the garbage bag over her head like a shelter. "One. Two. Three."

They both ran for the car at the same time. When she pulled her door closed, she was giggling and the sound of it set up a reverberation all the way to his toes. She had a nice laugh.

Just business, Brand.

He shoved the bag of stuff onto her lap as he opened the console drink holder and secured his coffee cup. She put hers in the holder beside his and brought the towel pack out of the bag. After tearing the packaging apart, she reached toward his head with a towel.

He could hardly say no since water was running from

his hair down his face and neck. Taking the towel he ran it over his head roughly. When it was drenched like a washcloth in the bathtub, he threw it into the rear floorboard.

"Guess that was a good idea." He grinned.

"You're welcome," she said. "Maybe finding a place to wait this out would be an even better idea."

"Under other circumstances, you'd probably be right."

He started the car and pulled away, taking a swig of his coffee. The little groan he released at the simple pleasure had Cami's nerve endings standing at attention.

When they were back on the road, he said, "So. Hand me the donuts and move on to Chapter Two."

She retrieved the bag of donuts.

"You sure you want to eat this stuff?"

He gave her a look indicating that her question wasn't worthy of an answer.

Brandon set the bag in his lap, took a bite of one of the donuts and licked his fingers.

"So where were we?"

"You found out from your friend that your groom was a fifth degree douche."

"Yes. I did. And he was. Is. We sailed around the British Virgin Islands for a week. It was lovely. I was on top of the world. Of course that was before any of the trouble started."

"Does the trouble include what you learned from the maid of honor?"

"Not really. If that was all there was to this…"

She seemed to get lost in thought before she finished the sentence.

Brandon sat quietly eating donuts, drinking coffee, and concentrating on the headlights finding the dotted center line. After a few minutes he said, "Hey. Did I lose you?"

"What? I, uh, no. Right here. Maybe I need therapy. Telling this stuff… It's not easy."

"Maybe you don't need therapy. Maybe you just need to get it out."

"You a nice guy, Brandon? I didn't peg you for a nice guy at first, but you're starting to seem like a nice guy."

"What do you know? You've got shit taste in men."

He grinned.

She laughed.

"That can't be denied."

"So keep going."

"Okay. I had a condo right on the Back Bay Fens. So I could just walk straight across the park to get to work. It was nice, even on bad weather days. I loved that condo. He had the penthouse at the Folio. That's in the financial district and he wanted to live there. When I said I'd like to stay near the museum, at first he laughed. He said, 'You can't think I'd consider moving into your quaint little flop, Camden'.

"There was a fight over where we were going to live. I said that, since he didn't walk anywhere, but kept a car and driver at his disposal, it didn't matter if he was a mile away from work. He said he couldn't entertain guests in a place like mine, that I needed to grow up and get serious about my real job – taking care of him.

"Now that I look back on things, I can see clearly that the tug of war over where we were going to live was a turning point. During that argument he made it clear that, not only did he intend for us to live at his place, which was decorated with an obscene lack of taste, but he'd also taken it for granted that I was going to give up my job and dedicate my life to planning and hostessing dinner parties.

"Of course I know how to do that. Everybody who grows up in my world knows how to do that. I just didn't have it in mind for me. It had never occurred to me that he'd expect me to give up my job. There are probably a thousand people in the world who would kill for that job. He'd always said how proud he was to be with somebody so cultured. It was just part of his pitch."

She opened the plastic tab that kept the lid of her coffee closed and took a drink. It was starting to get warm in the car again.

"So you moved to his place?"

"Yeah," she said, so quietly he almost didn't hear it over the rain. "I did everything he wanted. In the end I gave up my job. Moved to his place, but it never felt like a home. He'd had it 'done'…" she did air quotes with one hand, "by a New York designer who was brilliant and gay and brilliantly gay." Brandon sniggered. "So he didn't want me to make any changes. Moving was just the beginning though. The demands didn't stop there, but the more I agreed to, the more he wanted."

When she stopped talking, Brandon said, "Like what?"

"My isolation. He started finding reasons why he didn't like my friends. He felt like any attention given to them was attention that should have been focused on his needs.

"My clothes. He wanted me to play arm candy and, to him, that meant clothes more revealing than I was comfortable with.

"Everything became a point of contention, a reason to critique and pick at me. Long story short, I never did anything right.

"I never saw my family unless Trey was able to go with me and I knew that there would be hell to pay if they caught on to the fact that I wasn't happy. One day my doorman rang the intercom and said my father was downstairs. I was panicked. I couldn't let him come up because, ah, there was evidence of Trey's displeasure."

Brandon's jaw clenched even though he knew this part was coming.

"He hit you."

"Only when there were no command performances on the calendar for two weeks. Long enough for bruises to fade away.

"I told the doorman to let me speak with my dad. I said it wasn't a good time. He said he didn't care whether it was or not. He wanted to see me right then. We argued back and forth about it, but you know, he's one of those guys. Doesn't take no for an answer. You find a lot of those at the heads of big companies. He walked away from the doorman and called my cell.

"I told him I'd meet him for lunch, but didn't plan to actually go. The bruises on my face were new. Fresh from the night before. Trey had thought I drank too much wine at a dinner party. He let me know in graphic terms when we got home.

"Dad said one of my friends had come to see him. Roxanne Radcliffe. She was my roommate at the sorority house my last two years as an undergrad. I ran into her shopping and she could tell something was wrong. I guess if you live with somebody for two years they know you really well. My acting skills weren't up to the challenge of persuading her that I was okay. Apparently."

She rifled through the sack of stuff and pulled out the cranberry juice. She took a drink.

Brandon glanced over at her.

"Go easy on that. I'm not seeing Ladies Lounges every few yards out here and, between the *venti* coffee and juice…"

"Mind your own business."

He chuckled. She seemed to be growing more confident by the minute. He'd never thought he'd ever find the occasion to think the word 'spunky', but that was what popped up in his head.

"Don't cry to me when you can't hold it and don't have any place to go." He could feel her glare. "I'm just saying."

They drove without talking while she polished off the banana, each hearing his or her own thoughts and the relentless sound of rain.

"How far to the next town?" she asked.

"You're the navigator. You tell me."

"It's dark," she said.

He leaned over her and retrieved a palm-sized light from the glove box.

"Here. It's a miracle called batteries."

"Funny," she said drily. She opened the atlas and starting from the cottage, clearly marked with highlighter, estimated their location. "Jensing? About ten miles?"

"You don't sound too sure."

"That's because I'm not too sure. It's a guess."

"Here's a sign. See if you can read it."

He slowed down.

"Jensing! Eight miles!" She sounded so excited it was infectious.

He smiled. "See? You learned a new skill. You can navigate by flashlight."

"Bullet point for my resume," she said without emotion. "Which I guess is going to need updating." She attempted to mimic sounding bright and cheerful. "I can explain the gap in my work history. I took time off for abuse and serious downgrading of self-esteem'. But none of that will matter when I attempt to interview with platinum tips at the end of short spikey hair. I'll never get in the door."

"That's where you're wrong. A list of the right contacts trumps everything. Education. Experience." His eyes did a quick scan of her appearance. "Style."

She laughed. "You call this style?"

"Yeah. It may not be *Vogue*, but it's a look. Well, what do you know?"

"What?" She looked around to see if she could find a reference point for that question. When she came up empty, she asked again. "What?"

He smiled. "There's a Waffle House in three miles."

"No."

"Yeah. There is."

"I don't mean no, there isn't a Waffle House. I mean no, I'm not eating there."

"You're not?"

"No. I'm not."

"Too bad. You'll have to watch me."

She narrowed her eyes. "Can I have a blindfold?"

He chuckled. "No. We're trying to avoid calling attention to ourselves."

She gaped before pointing a finger at her head.

"Whoever came up with this hair suggestion didn't get the memo. In rural America I stand out like flashing red and blue lights."

It was still dark as charcoal gray outside because of the dense rainclouds, but the sun had come up and was giving off enough light for him to see the hair she was talking about.

"You have a point. I wasn't in on that part of the

planning."

"So you aren't the one to blame. Good to know."

"It's not that bad."

"Right."

"And the great thing is, hair grows. You can outlive any mistake."

Her eyes darted to his arm. "Unlike ink."

"I've heard you can undo ink, not that I have any intention of it."

"Did it hurt?"

"Like a motherfucker." He grinned at her.

"Why'd you do it?"

"What? Get the ink?"

"Yes."

Brandon sighed. "It's a story for another time." He smiled over at her. "Maybe someday." He put his foot on the brake and slowed even further. "And here we are."

There were three other cars in the parking lot. Because the day was so dark and the lights were so bright, Brandon could see inside the building and appraise the risk before they ever got out of the car. Instead of parking close to the front, he parked as close to the back door as possible, which meant it was also mostly hidden by the big garbage containers.

"It's garbage bag time," he said. When she was finished readying her plastic cover, he said, "The back door is probably locked. We can try it or run for the front."

"Back door," she said decisively and without hesitation.

Brandon smiled. She was a risk taker. Like him.

"On three. One. Two. Three."

They slammed the car doors and ran for the rear door. It was locked. Over the rain, he heard Cami giggle about the fact that they couldn't get in.

Once inside, the assistant manager welcomed them.

"Thanks," said Brand. "We'll take that booth in the back. The one right over there by the kitchen."

The manager nodded and handed them two menus, smiling.

"Sit where you want."

When Brandon took the side of the booth against the back wall, he was satisfied that he could see everything; the parking lot, the entire eatery, and part of the kitchen. Cami sat facing him, which meant she was facing away from everybody else. It wasn't as safe as a bunker, but it was as safe as breakfast was going to be on a Thursday morning near the Kentucky state line.

By the time they got their menus open the waitress was there with setups and coffee cups.

"You kids look half drowned. You want coffee?"

"Yes, please," Cami smiled up at her.

"Yeah. Thanks," Brandon said.

"Cream?"

"None for me. She'll have enough for both of us though." He didn't look up from his menu when he said it.

The waitress laughed and looked at Cami. "I like a little coffee with my cream, too, hon."

In a few seconds she was back with a cream pitcher and a coffee carafe. As soon as she filled the cups with steaming hot java Cami put both hands around her mug to warm them up.

"Hmmm," she said. "Now if I was only dry and warm and had a chance at a decent meal."

Brandon flipped his menu.

"This food is better than decent. It's *available*." He paused before adding, "Now."

"You make a good argument." She opened her menu and started to look around.

When the waitress came back, Brandon said, "I'll have the steak and eggs with hashbrowns, sunny side up, medium on the steak. Instead of toast bring me a grilled cheese sandwich cut in half."

She nodded and looked at Cami.

"Two scrambled eggs with tomatoes. Do you have wheat toast?"

"Yes, darlin'. We may be country folk, but we got wheat toast."

Cami wasn't sure how to respond.

"Um, can I have that, please? No butter?"

The waitress laughed, shook her head, and took the menus as she left.

"I think you made an impression on her," Brandon said.

Cami sighed. "I didn't mean any offense, but there was no mention of wheat bread on the menu."

Brand laughed. "You care what she thinks of you,

don't you?"

Cami's eyebrows drew down into a frown. "Are you implying that's a flag wave for low self-esteem?"

He shook his head as he scanned the parking lot for new arrivals. It seemed people with good sense stayed home on days when rain was pelting in sheets.

"No. I'm not saying that."

"I feel like I'll never be dry again."

"We'll find a place to stop for the night before it gets dark again."

She smiled slightly. "It's my turn to drive."

"I didn't agree to letting you drive."

"It's not safe for you to take on all the tension."

"How do I even know that you know how to drive? How many road trips have you taken?"

"I haven't taken any road trips before, per se, but I drive back and forth between the city and Weston. And that's a lot harder than what you've been doing out here in the…"

The waitress arrived with armloads of food just as Cami was about to make some disparaging remark about rural life.

After setting down all the food, she said, "Be right back with that grilled cheese."

"Looks good. Thanks," said Brandon.

"What's your last name?" Cami asked out of the blue.

"Why do you want to know?"

She shrugged. "You know mine."

"It's better if you don't know mine."

"Why's that? Because you're a secret ninja black ops spook who will fade into the wind after this job is over?"

Brandon stared at her for all of five seconds before breaking into full-on laughter that took her aback and pleased her at the same time. Real laughter was a good look on him.

"Yes. You have me dead to rights."

"So maybe Brandon isn't your real name."

"Maybe not. Okay. You can drive for a while. Do you always have sliced tomatoes with your eggs?"

"I wouldn't say always, but it's a good pairing. Why?"

He rolled a shoulder and stretched his neck as if to say he didn't care and couldn't figure out why he'd asked.

The waitress saved him from answering by returning with his grilled cheese.

"Do you always have steak, eggs, *and* a grilled cheese sandwich?" She laughed.

He smiled as he took a bite that equaled a quarter of the sandwich. When he was finished chewing, he took a drink of coffee before answering.

"No. I saw the grilled cheese on the menu. I wanted that *and* the steak and eggs."

"So you're a thinker outside the box."

"I hope so. I'm kind of surprised that we haven't visited the restrooms yet. I was thinking we have to check out every toilet between here and Austin."

"That's my goal. Don't worry. I'll have a travel guide report before we leave this fine establishment."

"Hmmm. Be sure you have a nice crisp folded bill to

leave the attendant."

Cami laughed.

"I really wish there was an attendant just so it would shock that smug look off your face."

True to her word, when they were finished, she asked the waitress where to find the 'ladies' room'.

"Back up to the front and take a right."

"I assume you're coming," Cami said to Brandon as she slid out of the booth. "I know the drill by now."

"Right behind you, Rose."

When Brandon opened the door to the women's room, he found that there were two stalls. Bending to peer underneath, he saw that one was occupied.

"You'll have to wait," he said.

"Why?"

"Somebody's in there."

"I'm sure it's a woman."

"Not up for discussion."

"For Christ's sake." She slumped against the wall in a huff that looked like a teenage protest.

It was intended to be a little rebellion, but Brandon thought it was kind of cute. He was also glad to see that the soon-to-be ex-husband hadn't completely broken her spirit. She was damaged, but not cowed.

When the woman who'd been in the restroom left, Brandon waved an okay for Cami to go in. As usual he was waiting and watching the door like the second coming would emerge, which she thought was kind of appealing. In its own way.

"Get your garbage bag," he said quietly. "I didn't know it was possible, but it might be raining harder."

"That's *not* possible."

"Judge for yourself." He nodded toward the glass front.

"You promise we'll stop before dark?"

"If we can find a place that looks safe."

CHAPTER FIVE

Tennessee

C AMI GOT BEHIND the steering wheel and fumbled to get the wet garbage bag off her. Brandon reached over to help. When he pulled it away, they were face to face and experiencing a connection neither of them was prepared for. He pulled his eyes away as he threw the garbage bag in the rear floorboard. He came back up with a pack of cotton hand towels. He reached toward her face with one of them. She took it, smiled gratefully, and rubbed it over her face and hair.

"I'm not sure the bag is doing any good. I'm wet through and through."

"I'm wishing I wasn't wearing jeans. I think they're starting to chafe."

"Ouch." She chuckled. "We could find a place to stop right now. Pull over. Get warm and dry. Watch TV."

"Nice try. Shut up and drive."

"Stop being so bossy. You work for me."

"No, Rose. I work for your daddy."

She waved a hand in the air as she backed out. "Whatever."

They continued southwest on the state highway. When visibility was as much as twenty feet they crawled along at twenty mph. At times the downpour was so hard they were forced to pull over and wait. The storm created a cocoon of intimacy as they sat side by side, both a little uncomfortable with the nearness of the other, each silently wondering if the attraction was one-sided. Cami telling herself that she couldn't possibly get involved with somebody whose background was so drastically different. They had nothing in common. Brandon telling himself that she was a means of earning cred in the club. Nothing more.

To break up the silence and create a distraction from the air that was feeling heavier in the SUV, Brandon said, "You've got a story to finish. You were saying that you told your father you'd meet him for lunch just to get rid of him."

"Wow. You've got a good memory."

"I know. So pick up where you left off."

She took a deep breath. "I was going to make a list for the housekeeper, but every pen I kept in the kitchen drawer had gone dry. I'd spent ten minutes drawing inkless swirls on paper. I went to Trey's study to borrow a pen and found one in the top drawer where you'd expect it to be. Trey is kind of anal about neatness."

Brand couldn't tell for sure, but he thought she might have been clenching her jaw when she said that last sentence.

"I was almost to the door when something made me

turn around. I can't explain it. I know it's going to sound like one of those crazy ESP things. Call it woman's intuition. But I had the feeling I should look through his drawers. The bottom drawer was locked.

"So I called downstairs to the doorman, Tony. I told him that I had accidentally locked my desk drawer and asked if he knew anybody who could open it. Right away. For cash. Without mentioning to my husband that I'd lost the key.

"Tony is agreeable and bright and, although he certainly never said so, I got the impression, call it woman's intuition, that he wasn't crazy about Trey.

"He said he might know somebody like that and said he'd call me back shortly. And he did. There was a guy there within the hour. I wasn't too worried about being discovered breaking into Trey's desk because he never came home during the day and, whenever I had visible bruises, the housekeeper got a week off.

"So Tony's guy was into the desk drawer within a minute. He waited while I had a look around and then put it back the way he found it. I gave him a hundred bucks cash and let him out."

She slowed down because the rain was surging.

"What was in the drawer?" Brand asked.

"A will. My will. And it was signed. I mean… not by me. But it was a perfect copy of my signature."

"A forgery?"

"Yes."

"Massachusetts is not a community property state."

She shook her head.

"No. The only way for him to *automatically* inherit everything that's mine would be for me to will it to him. And I really, really don't want this to come off like bragging, but my inheritance would be enough to tempt somebody who was greedy, without conscience or principle. I'm an only child and the family has been doing okay for a couple of generations."

"And by okay you mean top one percent of top one percent."

"Yes. That's what I mean. And that wasn't all he planned."

"Go on."

"I opened his laptop and pulled up search history. He'd been researching ways to commit suicide. Judging by the number of articles he'd read on the subject, he was most fascinated by the deadly combination of tequila and acetaminophen."

"He was going to have you sign a will leaving everything to him and then you were going to accidentally mix painkillers with tequila."

"Yeah. I was probably going to *accidentally* do that while he was at work because I was so distraught about walking into doors and falling down."

After a few minutes of silence, Brand pressed for more. "What did you do?"

"I grabbed a few things that had sentimental value and threw them into a bag. Along with the will. And more or less ran out of there. On the way down in the elevator I called my dad and told him to come pick me up. I waited downstairs because I knew one thing and that was that I never wanted to be alone with Trey again.

"You can imagine what my dad's reaction was when he saw me. I was afraid he was going to go after Trey himself."

"If I had a daughter, that's what I'd do. I think that's what most men would do."

"Well, I begged him not to. Not because I didn't think Trey deserved a taste of what I'd experienced, but because Trey's the sort who would press charges and then my family would be involved in a scandal. That kind of thing is bad for business and there are thousands of families who are counting on a paycheck that originates with my dad."

She sounded like she took the weight of that responsibility seriously. Brandon knew exactly what she was talking about. Few people ever had the chance to find out that it could be a burden to know that a lot of people were depending on you to make good decisions and practically predict the future. Accurately.

"I stayed at home, in Weston, while divorce proceedings were started. It felt good to be in the bedroom where I grew up. Comforting. Safe. You know? Scratch that. Of course you don't know. I can't see a guy like you ever feeling like a victim."

Brandon mulled that over as they inched along. It was true. He couldn't say that he'd ever felt victimized. In that respect he'd had a good life. For that matter, he'd had a good life in all respects, his only regret being that he hadn't grown up with his father and brother.

He cleared his throat.

"I can't put myself in your place, but I can understand why it would feel good to be back home."

"You can?"

"Yeah. I, ah, didn't know I had a father or a brother until…" He stopped like he was calculating, "about ten months ago."

"That sounds like a story."

"Right now we're talking about you. So go on."

"After he was served, I was ready to get on with my life. I'd never gotten around to selling my condo. So I moved back in. My plan was to look for another job while I was waiting for the divorce to come through.

"Then he started calling, saying he knew he'd made some mistakes. He wanted another chance. He hadn't talked to me like that since our wedding day."

"Talked to you like what?"

"Nice." They rode in silence for a few minutes before she said, "Maybe it would have worked if I still loved him, but I didn't. I changed my phone number and that's when his strategy got more intense. He started sending missives by courier."

Brandon lifted an eyebrow and smirked a little.

"Missives? That's a word I haven't heard much since the seventeenth century."

"Right. I mean letters."

"What did they say?"

"That if I didn't come back, where I belonged, there would be consequences. He didn't say what. Just left it to my imagination. But since I'd already suspected he was going to try to kill me for money, it didn't take a genius to figure out what he had in mind. I don't know why he didn't give it up once the plan was out in the open."

"If anything happened to you after you reported your suspicions to your father, the police would be at his door within minutes."

"Yes, but haven't you noticed that people with serious money never go to jail? Evidence disappears. Juries are compromised. Things happen behind closed doors. Under the table. In the shadows."

After a minute of silence, Brandon looked out the passenger window and simply said, "Yeah."

"It took a while for me to accept that he was capable of murdering me, but..." She paused. "He said things that scared me."

"It seems to me that the only thing he's holding over your head is a possible copy of a forged will, assuming that you took the original. Depending on how much he spent, the forgery might be good enough to stand up in court. So the way to invalidate that is to create a new will that postdates that one, have it witnessed by two reliable third parties and notarized, file it with the court, and put him on notice. In other words, render his motive impotent."

Cami looked back and forth between Brandon and the road several times before saying, "That seems...

perfectly reasonable. And flawlessly logical."

"I'm surprised your father didn't think of it."

"He may have. But I think, in the end, he also came to understand that Trey isn't…" she seemed to be searching for the right word, "…stable."

"Do you think he's crazy?"

She bit her bottom lip. "Yes."

Brandon looked perfectly sober.

"That explains why he wanted to steal you away and keep you someplace safe until after the divorce. But if it's more than money with this guy, how do you know he'll move on after the divorce?"

She shook her head. "I guess I don't. One step at a time. Right?"

"Right." Brandon regretted voicing his thoughts out loud without thinking about the effect his pessimism might have on her.

THEY DROVE ON and took turns with the radio. Brandon tried to lighten the mood by making fun of her musical taste. He made fun of the lyrics, the nasal twang, and the slide guitar. She did her best to defend her choice, but was often so overcome with laughter that she couldn't talk.

"So, let me see if I've got this straight. These songs are either about drinking, cheating, or love gone bad," he said.

When they stopped for gas and the ladies' room, Brandon took over driving again and commandeered the radio. At one point he got a little nervous about a pair of headlights following for twenty miles, but eventually they turned off and the lights disappeared.

"And what do you think rock is about?" She fired her own volley of musical critique. "Sex. Sex. More sex. 'Oh baby, I just can't keep my dick in my pants'."

Brandon laughed.

"Makes the world go round."

When it started getting darker in the late afternoon, she said, "You promised me a place where I can take a shower and put on dry clothes. With real food."

"I promised dry clothes. You made up the rest."

"Let's negotiate."

"What do you have that I want?"

"A turn on the radio."

"For what?"

"Stopping now."

The point became moot before he answered because the road ahead was barricaded. There were police cars with lights on blocking the way forward.

When Brandon pulled up, a sheriff's deputy in full rain gear walked over. Brandon lowered the window enough to ask, "What's going on?"

"The river's coming up over the bridge. You'll have to turn around."

"Okay. Thanks," Brandon said.

He turned around and started to backtrack.

"What now?" Cami said.

"I guess we'll see if we can get a room in the last town.

What was the name of it?"

"Claremoor."

By the time they made their way back to Claremoor it was dark, but even through the sheeting rain they could make out the bright pink neon VACANCY sign at the motel beside the road.

They pulled in under the overhang and went inside.

"We need two rooms. Connecting."

The clerk smiled like that was funny.

"There's a road block south of here. The bridge is out. Word's gotten around and people are scrambling for a place to stay. We've got one room with a queen-sized bed."

"We'll take it," Brandon said.

Cami was shaking her head vigorously.

"No. No, we won't."

"Yes. We will." Brandon did his best impression of an authoritarian figure, but it didn't faze her in the least. She continued shaking her head.

"Just a minute." He held up a finger to the clerk and pulled her aside. "What's the problem?"

She motioned between the two of them. "We can't share a room."

"Why not?"

"Because it would be extremely inappropriate and, I might add, unprofessional."

"You're worried that I may put moves on you." She looked a little offended that he sounded like the idea was preposterous. "You have no worries on that score."

She narrowed her eyes. "Oh really? And why's that?"

She was daring him to say she wasn't attractive or sexually desirable and he knew he'd have a hard time selling that. So what came out of his mouth next was even more preposterous.

"Because I'm not interested in girls." He knew she'd believe him because he was telling the truth. He wasn't interested in girls. He was interested in women. Like Camden Carmichael.

She took in a sharp breath. "You're gay!"

It was a statement, not a question, and said loud enough that the clerk looked their way with an amused expression.

Brandon watched her face as he neither confirmed nor denied.

"Well, that explains a lot," she said.

"What does that mean?"

"You're not bi?" she whispered.

He looked her directly in the eyes.

"I am definitely *not* bi. And what did you mean, 'that explains a lot'?"

Just then the bell over the door rang and another weather-weary traveler trudged in. Brandon sprang for the check-in counter to get there first and spread his arms like he was claiming the entire length of it.

"We'll take it," Brandon announced in no uncertain terms.

The clerk smirked and pushed a registration card across the counter for Brandon to fill out.

To the guy who'd just come in, he said, "Sorry, man. Last room's gone."

"But the sign…" The clerk switched the neon sign to NO VACANCY. "Try Morgansville. Maybe they have something."

"Morgansville?" The latecomer frowned. "How far is that?"

"Twenty-two miles north. Turn left at the first light. That's Highway 429."

Cami almost felt sorry enough for the guy to offer him a spot on the floor of their room.

"Where can we get something to eat?" Brandon asked.

"The Golden Griddle should be open for your dining pleasure. Three blocks down on the left. Next to the bank."

"Golden Griddle," Cami said drily.

Brandon took the key then took Cami by the elbow and ushered her out. "Were you expecting pho or a hummus bar?"

She groaned and the sound caused Brandon's cock to twitch. "Don't tease me like that."

When they got back in the car, Brandon said, "Okay. Here are the choices. We can go to Golden Griddle, sit down and eat, then come back to the motel and get dry. Or we can go to Golden Griddle, get to go, then come back to the motel, get dry, and eat in the room."

"Door number two."

He nodded and started the car.

Golden Griddle was open for business and they did get sopping wet, again.

When a concerned-looking woman approached them, Brandon said, "Can we get dinner to go?"

"Sure can," she said cheerfully. She handed them both menus.

"What's fast?" he asked.

"Most anything except steak," she said.

Brandon turned to Cami and repeated, "Most anything except steak," as if that was news and she was hard of hearing. His lips twitched at the corners when she made a face.

They sat on a vinyl bench and waited for club sandwiches, waffle fries, strawberry cheesecake.

The food was packed in Styrofoam containers, inside paper sacks, inside plastic bags.

"I put plastic bags around this so it won't get wet and soggy. Plastic ware and napkins are inside."

"Perfect. Thank you," Brandon said as he took the bags from her.

BRANDON BACKED THE SUV up so that the hatch back was right in front of their door. When the hatch was lifted it provided a sheltering bridge between the car and the porch overhang. That meant the luggage made it into the room without getting wet.

It was the usual motel setup. Bed. Two nightstands. Desk. Chair. TV. Seventies décor that had needed updating for thirty-five years. Or more. Everything within was old and tired, but on inspection, it seemed reasonably clean.

Cami began rifling through one of her bags.

"Shower before food and I claim it first."

"Okay, but hurry up. I'm liking the idea of some hot water myself."

She waved a hand by her shoulder in acknowledgement without looking up. When she located what she was looking for in her suitcase, she set it aside. She removed her hoodie and boots, then pulled her knit shirt over her head. When she turned to face Brandon, she was standing there in a flesh-colored, see-through lace bra that showed off her unimaginably perfect tits in the most beguiling way.

"Oh my God. I'm *so* sorry," she said, looking mortified.

Schooling his features to look as nonchalant as possible, he dropped his backpack in front of his crotch to hide his reaction to the exhibition standing in front of him, making his mouth water. It would be a sure giveaway that her misimpression regarding his sexual orientation was far afield of reality. He'd led her to a faulty conclusion and was stuck with it for the duration. After cursing himself for stupidity, he had to replay what she'd just said in his head a couple of times to settle on an answer that sounded like his brain was working.

"About what?"

"What I said about the New York designer. I didn't mean anything."

Brand managed a smile.

"I don't have thin skin and that guy probably plays up the flame because most muggles think that the more fabulous you are, the more creative you are." His eyes flicked downward and he smiled more broadly. "Pretty bra. I can see you have an appreciation for fine lingerie."

Looking down she ran her hands down the sides of her breasts, which almost brought him to his knees.

"Thanks. I like this one, too. Muggles?"

He swallowed hard. "It means…"

"I know what it means. I'm just surprised you do."

"Got dragged to one of the movies by a friend."

"Uh huh."

When she reached to unzip her jeans, Brandon decided it would be an ideal time to step outside and make phone calls on the porch. He turned away, dropped the backpack on the floor, and left the discomforting sight of Cami Carmichael in pretty things made of see-through lace.

He called his lawyer first and gave him detailed instructions on drawing up a new will for Cami.

Then he called Brant.

"Yeah?"

"It's Brand."

"I know. I gave you that phone."

"Right. We need a Plan B on this leg."

"What's up?"

"An unfortunate weather pattern. We've lost an entire day to heavy rain sitting right on top of us. Had to stop in Claremore, Tennessee because of high water. Bridge is closed to the south. You think you can find a local pilot who's instrument rated and willing to fly us out of this?"

"Hold on."

After a few minutes, Brant came back on the line.

"That weather's headed this way and it's big as the great state of Texas. You're going to have to head west to get out of it. We want you to keep moving. It's the safest thing."

"I know."

"Call you back with details."

"Yep."

Brandon heard the ended call beeps. He'd had a chance to survey the motel while he was on the phone. He'd walked the length of the porch. There were vehicles parked in front of every room, but none seemed unusual. Of course that wasn't a conclusive inference. After all, their vehicle seemed innocuous.

Every room had lights on, curtains drawn. A motel like that one was a security nightmare, but it couldn't be helped. He'd sleep facing the door, the Smith and Wesson with Crimson Trace under his pillow. It was a great gun for shooting while sleepy because the laser took accuracy of aim off the table. Point and pull. End of story.

WHEN HE REENTERED the room, he heard that the shower was still running. He turned on the TV to check stock prices. He'd been antsy about being out of touch with business for two days. He stood in front of the TV partly because he was tired of sitting down and partly because he didn't want his damp clothes to get the bed wet.

The pipes made high-pitched noises of protest when she turned the water off. He took that as a cue to get his own dry clothes together. So he unzipped his athletic bag and pulled out a pair of clean black knit boxers, a long-sleeve cotton tee, and the oldest softest jeans he owned.

When Cami emerged from the steamy bathroom, she looked good enough to eat. Her cheeks were flushed and shiny and, unlike a lot of women, she looked damn good without any makeup at all. She was wearing a different pair of flannel pajama bottoms and a short-sleeved cropped tee shirt that looked soft as sin.

She smiled brightly. "All yours."

Brandon nodded and started toward the bathroom when he realized that he couldn't go into the bath and turn on the shower while leaving Ms. Carmichael alone in the motel room. Unguarded. He stood still for a minute tapping his fingers against his thigh.

When she noticed that he hadn't moved, she said, "What's wrong?"

"You're not going to like this."

"Well, what else is new?"

He rolled his eyes. "Everything's relative."

"Just put it out there."

"I want a shower. No. I *need* a shower."

"Yeah. I know."

"I can't leave you alone out here."

She stared at Brandon with a blank look on her face for several seconds before breaking into laughter that warmed his blood like fine whiskey.

"Well, don't be shy. I'll watch you take a shower. A good beefcake show might be just what I need to relieve the monotony of rain pounding on metal."

Brandon gaped. That response was the last thing he'd expected. He tried to imagine having this woman, the one he was developing a craving for, watch him take a shower.

"Just so you know. I usually shower without any clothes on."

She looked at him like he might be slow. "Yeeeees. I suspected that."

He thought he'd had some unusual sexual encounters, but the accursed homosexual charade was turning into a bigger calamity at every turn. If there was a way out of it, he couldn't find it. So he decided to put on his big boy pants, or, ah, take them off, and be mature about it. After all, it wasn't like he was ashamed of his body.

He put on the least sincere smile of his entire life and said, "Glad you're not going to give me trouble."

"Trouble? No indeed. I can hardly wait." She waved toward the bath. "Let's get to it so we can eat. Instead of dinner and a show, it will be a show then dinner."

The way she laughed had him hating the idea of being the 'show'. Christ. Was that what it felt like to be objectified?

He could see that she was genuinely enjoying herself

and thought he might be witnessing devilish Cami.

Devilish.

Surprising.

Sexy.

Fun.

Smart.

And damaged.

SHE FOLLOWED HIM into the bathroom, closed the door behind her, then closed the toilet seat, sat down and crossed her legs. There she sat swinging one leg in anticipation, smiling like the Cheshire cat.

"You're not making this easy," he said.

"Payback's a bitch," she said.

"What am I being paid back for?" he asked.

"Well, let's see. Waking me up with a pillow to the head. Making me travel in wet pajama bottoms all day because you didn't give me time to dress this morning, much less shower. Then there was the music."

"Alright. Alright. I get the picture."

The bath was smaller than most broom closets. The shower was a standard three by three feet. The rest of the room was just big enough for a sink, toilet and one person.

Brandon pulled the flimsy vinyl curtain out of the way, turned on the water and waited until the temperature was right. The whole time he was silently chanting an affirmation that he would not let her see how awkward he felt about undressing in front of her.

When he pulled the wet Henley and tee shirt off over his head, Cami surpassed smiling and openly leered at his exposed upper body.

"What possessed you to cover half your body in all this color?" Brandon raised an eyebrow. "Not that it isn't attractive. I mean, I can see the appeal. But didn't it hurt?"

"Yes. It hurt."

He continued undressing, ignoring the question about why he would do that to his body. He just didn't feel like getting into the whole tale of matching his brother so he could get to know his dad incognito.

He tried to drop his wet pants, but they stuck to his legs and fought being removed.

"Here," she said. "Let me help."

"What happened to the person who was adamantly opposed to sharing a room because of the appearance of impropriety?"

"That was before I knew that it was just us girls." She smiled.

"Now wait a minute…"

From her makeshift grandstand she peeled at the jeans until she'd pushed them to the floor. Naturally, between that and the act of exposing himself to Cami, he was sporting the biggest erection of his entire life. He thought about trying to hide it, but realized there was no way in that proximity. The only thing he could do was own it.

When he pushed the boxers down and stood up, his

full and protruding glory was just twelve inches from her face and looking like it was trying to pull the rest of his body forward.

"I think this establishes the fact that this is not 'just us girls'."

Camden's eyes were wide and the smile had left her face. She swallowed, not able to pull her gaze away. It seemed that Brandon had been hiding what was without a doubt a penis intended for a god, the standard by which all others would be measured for all time. It was long, thick, straight and of a color that was pleasingly pink. The thick veins were not a detraction, but rather suggested an enhanced virility.

She could have wept thinking that such a work of art would be reserved for other men. It wasn't fair. It simply wasn't fair. But as Trey had loved to say as often as possible, life is not fair.

"Criminy, bodyguard. You've got a devilish body. If you weren't into boys…" She didn't finish the sentence, but the rest of the sentiment was obvious.

Brandon renewed his internal dialogue with a whole new string of colorful expletives.

"Don't be flattered. I always get excited about hot showers," he lied. He stepped under the water and pulled the curtain closed.

"Awwwww. Don't close the curtain. If you're going to jack off, I want to watch."

"You know," he said from inside the shower, "I'm starting to wonder if you were really raised to be a proper young lady."

Her response was a throaty, husky laugh that would do any barmaid proud. Indeed he was going to jerk off and he did not want her watching.

"I went to finishing school when I was fourteen. I can set a table for a seven course meal and tell you what kind of flowers to use for the centerpiece for any occasion. You can't produce a piece of flatware or cutlery that can stump me. I know what each one is and how to use it. I know how to sit, stand, walk – especially how to walk downstairs, how to do hair and, given my current circumstances, that's kind of funny, how to apply makeup for any and every occasion. I know when an event should be semiformal, black tie, and white tie. I know how to plan a party, how to treat guests, and how to keep conversation moving at dinner. Oh, yeah, I was raised to be a proper young lady. And I'd still love to see you jerk off."

By the time she was finished with that resume detailing how and why his mother would love her and why she'd be the perfect match for the head of St. Germane Enterprises, he'd come and the semen had already washed down the drain. He used the cheap motel shampoo, lathered himself with soap, and enjoyed the warmth of the water.

"That's impressive. Keep talking. I need to know you're still here."

"I'm here, but it's so steamy I'm practically wet again. And you promised me dry."

He turned off the water.

"Okay. I'm done." He opened the curtain and said, "Hand me a towel."

Her eyes flicked downward like a magnet as she reached for the towel and handed it to him. When she saw that his penis was flaccid, she smirked, opened the door and left. She didn't want to give him the satisfaction of knowing she thought he was still remarkable, even when soft.

The cold air that rushed into the bath almost made him gasp.

Damn that woman.

He was briskly rubbing the towel over his hair when the phone rang. He'd left it precariously perched on the two-inch ledge around the sink.

"Hello."

"What's the matter?" Brant asked in his voice that came out as either a soft growl, for his mother, or a loud growl, for everybody else.

"There's nothing the matter."

"Then why do you sound irritated?"

"I'm not irritated. I'm just getting out of the shower. I want to dry off and put on clothes."

After a pause, Brant said, "What did you do with the girl when you were in the shower?"

Brandon's teeth clenched together so hard he was afraid he was going to chip them all. "I made her sit on the toilet so I could keep an eye on her."

After another lengthy pause Brant broke into laughter. He wasn't sure he'd *ever* heard his father laugh that hard.

"And that didn't bother her?" Brant said, still chuckling.

"Not at all."

"Well, son, if the sight of a Fornight naked doesn't bother a girl, you're doing something wrong."

"She isn't bothered because she thinks I'm..." He turned away and cupped his hand over the phone to muffle his voice because the bath door was standing open to the bedroom, "...not straight."

"You mean she thinks you're lying? Not telling it straight?"

Brandon gritted his teeth. "No. That's not what I mean."

It took a minute for Brant to run through the list of other possibilities. When Brand's meaning finally registered, he started laughing all over again.

"Things got complicated," Brandon said defensively.

"Well, Jesus, son. I'm just glad you're taking this seriously."

Brandon wasn't sure if that was sarcastic or not. "Was there a reason why you called?"

"You mean other than to be thoroughly entertained? Yeah. Head back north into Kentucky in the morning and find the private airfield for Taylor County. Ask for a guy named Travis. He's gonna fly you over to New Mexico. To Poco Loco. I know a rancher with a private airstrip on his property. There'll be a car waiting for you. Stay in touch."

"Okay."

"Oh. Your mother has a pink feather thing she wears just to drive me crazy. If you'd like to borrow…"

Brandon ended the call and almost threw the phone.

HE PULLED ON his clean, *dry* clothes and stepped into the bedroom. Cami was sitting cross-legged on the bed with the food spread out, watching *Blood Sport*.

She had a quarter of a club sandwich in her hand and was chewing happily. "Sorry. I couldn't wait. After I finally got clean and dry I was able to focus on other things, like the fact that I'm starving."

Brandon lifted an eyebrow. "Jean-Claude Van Damme?"

She grinned sheepishly. "It's true. I'm a fan."

He shook his head. "You're full of surprises, Rose."

"You can call me Cami when we're alone, can't you?"

"I could, but then I might forget when we're getting gas or food or whatever. Safest to just think of you as Rose."

"Rose White," she corrected.

He sat down on the space she'd left on the bed and opened up containers. He picked up a waffle fry.

"Those are cold," she said.

"They'll be okay with ketchup."

She made a soft sound of amusement.

He glanced at the TV. "So you like Van Damme?" She nodded. "Name another one of his movies."

"Ooh. A pop quiz. Okay. *Universal Soldier*."

"You're cherry picking. Give me something less well known."

"Okay. My personal favorite. *Cyborg*."

Brandon looked genuinely impressed. "Okay. How about some trivia? Did you know he did one of the voices in the *Kung Fu Panda* movies?"

She gaped. "Shut up."

He chuckled. "No, really."

"You can't crush my crush with tales of animation."

"Oh. So it's a crush?"

"Well, duh. I'll bet the attraction is something we share. Isn't it? Tell the truth."

Brandon had no idea how a gay man would respond to that. "His roundhouse kick is to die for."

She laughed. "Yeah. That and everything else."

They sat and watched the rest of the movie in silence, polishing off the sandwiches, cold fries, and cheesecake.

"I grudgingly admit that bad food is good food. I'm stuffed, but happy. I'll think about damage control tomorrow."

"Speaking of tomorrow, we have to leave early. So get ready for lights out."

"Why do we have to leave early?" she said as she gathered up the to go trash and threw it away.

"Alternate plan. The good news is that we're going to get out of this rain."

"Okay. Which side of the bed do you want?"

"The side closest to the door." He said it slowly and deliberately like she was retarded.

"Are you a Gemini? Because you flip back and forth between sweet guy and asshole too often and too easily for normal."

As a matter of fact, he *was* a Gemini. So he did the only thing he could do and save face. He changed the subject by taking off his jeans. He kept on the boxers and the long-sleeve tee and pulled the covers back.

"I'm tired. I hope you don't snore," he said.

"I don't snore. And I hope you don't kick and hog covers."

"I don't."

"Good."

He was lying on his right side, facing the door, when he felt the bed move as she got in on her side. She switched off the bedside lamp, which momentarily plunged the room into darkness, but within a couple of minutes their eyes had adjusted and the light seeping in around the window curtain made everything in the room distinctly visible.

"Good night." She said it in a small voice that reminded him that, regardless of her bravado, she was a woman who was running scared.

It wasn't hard to make his voice sound comforting. He did want to give her comfort, make her feel safe.

"Good night, Rose."

He lay awake in the darkness for a while listening to the relentless rain. It didn't take long for her breathing to become even. He could feel her body generating heat under the covers they both shared. Truthfully, a queen-size bed wasn't very big once somebody his size was occupying half of it, or more.

The first conscious thought that made its way to his awareness was the strangest sense of well-being, like everything was okay with the world. If that had ever happened before, he didn't remember. The cause was immediately evident. Sometime during the night Cami had taken refuge against his body and was spooned to his back like she'd been made to fit there. Perfectly.

The conflict was excruciating. On the one hand, he knew he should get up and get started. On the other hand, the feeling of being cocooned in a magical spell was too wonderful to give up without first savoring just a little. In the end the decision was snatched away from his control.

Cami stirred awake, realized where she was and what she was doing and, thinking he was asleep, rolled away saying, "Jesus, Cam. What are you thinking?" under her breath.

Brandon waited until she was asleep again before getting up. He took care of bathroom essentials and dressed before waking her.

The motel was cheap, but they were kind enough to provide a functioning coffee maker with two paper cups, two lids, and two plastic sleeves of sweetener, creamer, and stir stick.

He threw the pillow from his side of the bed at her head and said in a voice that sounded every bit as gruff as Brant's, "Rise and shine! I'm making coffee to go. And you've got ten minutes to get the lead out."

She groaned. "This pillow throwing thing has lost all trace of amusement." She rolled over and looked at him with sleepy eyes that caused him to imagine crawling back in to spend the day in bed with Cami making love and listening to the rain. Of course first he'd have to explain how she'd wrongly concluded that he wasn't heterosexual and that could definitely be a mood killer.

He turned his back as he used bottled water to fill up the little coffee maker reservoir. "Nine and a half minutes."

"Okay. So it's Mr. Hyde this morning and not Dr. Jekyll. Whatever, Brandon."

She didn't quite slam the door to the bathroom, but she did punctuate that sentence by closing it soundly. He appreciated every little show of protest he drew from her. Perhaps one day she'd be a woman who didn't flinch when a man reached for the visor on her side of the car.

CHAPTER SIX

New York

RICHARD HILLFORT HAD been Severn Carmichael's executive assistant for fifteen years. During that time he'd come to appreciate the rarified air of billionaire lifestyles.

At the same time, Severn Carmichael had come to not only appreciate Richard, but to rely on him like the ground under his feet. Richard suspected that Mr. Carmichael might even love him like a son. After all, on Monday mornings Mr. Carmichael always inquired as to whether or not he'd enjoyed his weekend, on occasions when he'd actually had a weekend off.

That was all well and good, but Richard had gradually come to realize that it wasn't ever going to get him a yacht, or a seat on the board, or even his own office.

He'd come to realize that, when he was invited aboard yachts, it was to serve the administrative needs of Mr. Carmichael. There was no room for someone in his position to advance. He was already at the top of his occupation with a lot of unsatisfied ambition.

Of course Mr. Carmichael trusted him implicitly.

He'd sooner doubt the Pope than Rich Hillfort.

Trey Michaels had a gift for discerning unfulfilled desires. Like a computer he could analyze a person's carriage, or eye movements, or hand gestures, and accurately pinpoint what that person was missing in his or her life. It was an uncanny ability that had served him beautifully and, perhaps, was largely responsible for his financial success. Unlike most of the men at the City Club, he hadn't inherited a thing except for a proclivity for bending rules to suit him.

When Trey Michaels realized that Cami wasn't coming back, and that his wealth, power, and influence weren't going to grow exponentially by benefitting from a spousal inheritance shortcut, he went through the stages of a foiled plan.

Surprise.

Disbelief.

Bargaining.

Anger.

Revenge.

He wasn't just angry about the loss of potential wealth. He was livid about the idea of being bested. He could not lose to his soon-to-be ex-wife. He *would* not lose to his soon-to-be ex-wife.

It didn't matter what it cost him. He had to be the winner. Nothing less was acceptable. Sitting in the dark in the penthouse he'd once shared with Camden, he hatched a plan featuring Rich Hillfort as the lynchpin.

The next morning he phoned Heather Rebus. She was

one of Mr. Carmichael's three administrative assistants. She was a flamboyant orangey redhead who liked to wear red dresses, red lipstick, and stud earrings that always drew his attention because they were pearls far too big to be real, at any price.

When he'd first married Cami, Heather had made a point of flirting with Trey every time he went to see Carmichael. Not innocent flirting or romantic flirting, but fuck-me flirting. So he did.

Repeatedly.

Until he was tired of it and tired of her. But he'd managed to not burn the bridge by telling her that his wife was getting suspicious. He hated to give up his rendezvous, but what could he do? He was a married man.

The next morning he called her number. The contact had been disguised on his phone as Heath Inc.

"Mr. Carmichael's office."

"Heather, darling," Trey purred.

"Hey, baby." She dropped her voice as if she was talking to a lover. He almost rolled his eyes.

"How are you?"

"Not wearing any underwear if that's what you're asking. I heard you may soon be single."

"Indeed. And when I am, guess who I'm calling first?"

She giggled. "Hope that's me."

"Who else?" he said. "I've got to go, but I'll be in touch."

"Okay."

"Oh, I almost forgot. Is Carmichael going to be out of town anytime soon?"

"I can look. Why?"

"I don't want him to see me surprise you at work. You know. I was married to his daughter."

"Surprise me at work?" She sounded breathless. "Let me look." After a brief pause, she said, "He's going to the house at Kennebunkport on the twenty-second."

"Good girl. See you soon."

He ended the call wondering how God could have made women who were so gullible.

AT PRECISELY 10 a.m. on the twenty-second, Trey called Richard Hillfort.

"Hillfort," he answered.

"Hello, Rich. It's Trey."

"Yes. I see that. You're still in my contacts."

"Right. I was wondering if you might get free for lunch?"

Richard was immediately guarded. Michaels had been around for over two years and had never given him the time of day. "Lunch?"

"Yes. If you must know, I want to proposition you. I've always admired your service to Carmichael. Professional. Efficient. Precise. Give me an hour of your time and let me pitch working for me. Doesn't cost a thing to listen. Right?"

"Perhaps." Trey could hear suspicion dripping from Hillfort's tone, but he knew before he ever made that call that curiosity would win out in the end.

"I'm checking out 33 Arch today. I'm thinking about taking some space there. Meet me on the thirty-third floor at one and we'll have a private lunch."

A private lunch on the thirty-third floor? Rich knew he was going to say yes. He couldn't turn it down. After all, he'd just been thinking that he'd reached a career dead end. But maybe not.

In his head, he was already making a preliminary list of perks he'd ask for to negotiate a contract to work for Michaels, whom he found distasteful, but there were lots of things more important than personality.

"Isn't that the same building the Securities and Exchange Commission is in?" Richard asked.

"Hmmm. Not sure. Why?"

Of course Trey knew it was the same building that housed the SEC. Trey never did anything without purpose.

"No reason. Of course I will join you for lunch so long as we agree that the conversation is not only private, but also confidential."

"Certainly. That's why I picked a place where we won't be seen together."

"Alright. Looking forward to it."

"See you at one."

Trey ended the call and smiled.

ONE OF THE things he loved about being rich was that money could make almost anything happen. He couldn't trust leaving the details of the meeting to anyone else.

He personally called Déjà Vu Catering, he'd seen their trucks parked at some of the biggest society events and knew they were top shelf. When he explained that he needed gourmet lunch delivered and served with the best china, linens, crystal, and silver that could be rented, they laughed. Until he mentioned how much he was willing to spend.

Trey Michaels had a courier deliver cash in an envelope. The caterer probably interpreted that as a signal to mean that the client, who'd given the name of John Bigliogi, was flying below the radar. Like a lot of people, they didn't examine the ethics of cash too closely. And like a lot of people, they gave even better service to people who paid cash.

He'd been to 33 Arch Street the day before and made arrangements with building management to have exclusive use of the top floor for an hour and a half to serve lunch to members of the board. After dazzling the young lady who showed him the space with sex laden charm, a phony business card and hints about his growing real estate needs, she was happy to accommodate.

He accepted the key from the management office at 12:15 and met Déjà Vu Catering on the top floor at 12:30. By the time Richard arrived for the lunch meeting, a table was set in a huge corner office with a breathtaking view of the Boston Commons and Charles River beyond.

The caterer had exceeded expectations.

The table was covered in crisp white linen. The china

was heavy and white with an understated double gold rim. The white wine was chilled on ice. And a mass of orange lilies packed into a clear square vase formed a low centerpiece that looked like prosperity come to life.

A side table was set up with tossed salad and hot dishes under warmer domes.

Trey wasn't surprised when he heard the elevator ding at precisely one o'clock. Richard was a stickler for punctuality, a fine trait for someone in his position.

"Come in." Trey smiled.

The entire floor was empty. Not a stick of furniture, but it was clean and pristine with new carpet and paint recent enough to be called fresh, but not so recent as to be unpleasantly smelly.

Richard shook Trey's extended hand then followed him to the office where lunch was set up. One look at the view and Richard said, "I see why you'd want to office here. That's impressive."

"Yes. Well. As it turns out, we won't be moving here. Got word that they're going to transform this building into hotel/condos at the end of this year. The bottom ten stories will be hotel. The top thirteen will be condos. This floor will be divided into four condos. The view is first come, first served, of course."

"So you're thinking about *living* here."

Trey gestured for Richard to sit down. "I may be interested in purchasing one of these units. I like this view the best. Of course they'll build it out with whatever the new owner stipulates as far as fixtures and aesthetics."

He tossed the salad a couple of times, put some on a salad plate and set it down in front of Richard.

"Thank you," he said, feeling a little uncomfortable with the idea of being literally served by Trey Michaels. He waited patiently, or as patiently as possible, for Michaels to seat himself with his own salad plate.

"How long have you been with Carmichael?"

"Fifteen years."

"Are you happy with your job there?" Trey set his salad plate down and proceeded to pour wine for Richard and then himself.

"Mostly."

"Mostly," Trey repeated almost absently. One word that spoke volumes and left the door wide open for negotiation. He sat down and picked up his salad fork. "Is your dissatisfaction with the work itself or with the station in life where you've found yourself stymied?"

Richard felt a little irritated that Michaels evidently saw right through what he'd believed was an impenetrable mask of composure. Not to mention that the use of the term 'stymied' was rather insulting.

"I didn't say I was dissatisfied."

"No, you didn't. But to me, satisfaction means being able to answer that question with a word like 'completely'. Not mostly." He took a bite of salad then lifted his wine glass, looking at Richard as if he was studying his reaction. "So, if the answer isn't 'completely', then what is it that's coming up short? Work or lifestyle?"

Richard thought about that for a minute. He didn't

waste time contemplating either of those questions since he'd believed himself to be, as Michaels had rightly put it, 'stymied'.

"If I was forced to answer, I'd probably say both. That I'd like new challenges at work and better remuneration."

Trey nodded thoughtfully. "You know it's no accident that you're here with me today. For the past couple of years I've had the opportunity to observe how valuable you are."

It would have been impossible for Richard not to respond to that sort of praise and recognition. He'd been unaware that he'd ever made a lasting impression on Mr. Carmichael's associates, or extended family.

"That's very flattering."

"I don't flatter, Hillfort. If it wasn't true, I wouldn't say it," he lied. "The fact is that I believe you're capable of much more. You're being underutilized."

"Nice of you to notice."

"Not at all."

Trey rose, took away the salad plates, placed the entrees on the china chargers and removed the stainless covers. Pecan crusted chicken breast fillets with poached tomatoes.

"Smells good," Richard said. "And looks incredibly healthy."

"You only get one body per life, right?"

Richard looked at him with open curiosity, but replied, "Right."

"I don't think I've ever asked if you're married."

"No. I've never been married."

"Girlfriend?"

Richard smiled a little. "Sometimes. Nothing regular or lasting. I seem to become less attractive when women realize the extent of demand that my work requires. Most nights. Most weekends."

"That's no way to live, Richard." Richard could think of no reply to that. "So let's talk hypotheticals. I'm not claiming to be your personal genie, but I do have it in my power to change your life for the better.

"What if I was to offer you the deed to this condo? Twice your current salary and a contract that says you will work no more than fifty hours a week. Ever."

Richard had frozen with a bite of chicken two inches away from his mouth. He lowered his fork, but didn't close his mouth. "I would wonder what I have to offer that would be *that* valuable."

"Very perceptive of you, Rich. As it happens, there is something you could do for me as a show of good faith, while you're still with Carmichael."

All of Richard's internal warning signals were going off. But he couldn't stop himself from asking the question. "What?"

"Well, as you know, my wife and I are separated. What you may not know is that I love my wife. I'd do anything to get her back. *Anything.* Which means that information about her whereabouts is at a premium. I can't beg her to forgive me if I can't find her and, right now, her father is hiding her from me."

Richard sat up. "You want me to spy on Mr. Carmichael?"

"Well, let's not be dramatic. As his top assistant, you're privy to information. It's not like I'm somebody who intends her harm. Until a judge says otherwise, I'm her husband. You could be the hero in this scenario. Helping to patch up a lovers' quarrel.

"I just want you to find out where she is and let me know. Simple. Easy. With a gigantic return on your investment."

Richard looked out at the view of the Commons again before saying, "I'd like to think about it."

"Of course. The offer is open until this time tomorrow. Then it goes away." Richard got up and started for the door. "You're welcome to stay for dessert."

"No. Thank you."

"And, Richard. No one knows that you and I had this meeting. Likewise, no one is ever to know. Are we clear?"

"Yes, sir, Mr. Michaels."

"Good. I'll look forward to hearing from you tomorrow and I trust the news will be good. Find a pay phone somewhere and contact me at this number. The earlier, the better. Time is a consideration." He handed Richard a card. "I'd like you to memorize the number while you're here with me."

Richard took the card, studied it for a minute, then handed it back.

CHAPTER SEVEN

Kentucky Part Deux

CAMI HELD HER coffee in both hands. It was still raining. She didn't get drenched between the motel door and the car, but she wasn't completely dry anymore either.

"So what now?" she asked.

"Back to Kentucky." He handed her the atlas and pointed to a tiny airplane symbol encircled by orange highlighter. "We're going there."

"We're flying somewhere? Thank God!" She looked over at him. "Somewhere out of the rain. Right?"

"That's the plan."

"Where? I hope it's a desert where it hasn't rained in decades."

He chuckled because she wasn't far off. He was sure it had rained sometime that year, but at the same time, New Mexico wasn't exactly tropical.

"What's funny?" she asked.

"We're going to Poco Loco in New Mexico and we're not likely to see any rain once we get there."

She closed her eyes and moaned with longing. "I can't

wait."

"Come on. It hasn't been *that* bad."

She looked at him with wide eyes. "It's not that bad when you're warm and dry. And asleep. But riding in a car all day with wet clothes goes on my list of things never to do again."

He couldn't really argue that. "You want sit down breakfast enough to get wet or you want to go through a McDonalds drive through?"

As far as Cami was concerned, that was a painful and unfair choice between two evils. Probably. But maybe she should keep an open mind.

"What do they have?"

"McDonalds?"

"Yes."

He looked at her incredulously. "Seriously?" She made a face. "They have biscuits with sausage and pancakes, although I wouldn't really recommend those. The best thing is an English muffin with a piece of ham, a poached egg, and cheese."

"That doesn't sound too bad."

"Excellent choice. There's only one problem."

"What?"

"All the McDonalds are in the big towns or on the interstates."

"Great."

"So what will it be? Get wet and get food at the local café or drive for a while?"

"Why? Because you think we might drive out of the

rain? Let's get food."

"How's your garbage bag holding up?"

"It will outlast the pyramids. You should have taken one for yourself."

"Hindsight," he said.

When they pulled into the town square they saw a string of cars parked by a movie theater that had probably been closed for forty years.

"That's got to be it."

"What?" Cami was getting very tired of asking 'what' and 'why' every other minute, but Brandon had a way of making statements that begged for questioning.

"Breakfast. Get your bag on." She pulled the bag up and held it clenched at her neck so that it covered her head, shoulders, and upper body. "You ready?" She nodded. "One. Two. Three."

They opened their doors and ran for the overhang as fast as they could. When they stepped inside, the locals gave them both a good looking over before turning back to their solitary breakfasts or their conversations.

"Sit anywhere," said a woman who passed by carrying a coffee carafe. She was wearing an apron over jeans and tennis shoes so they assumed she knew what she was talking about.

Brandon motioned toward a booth in the back. As soon as they sat, the waitress was there.

"Coffee?" she asked.

"Yeah," said Brand.

"No," said Cami. "I just had some. Thank you."

"Sure." She placed two menus in front of them. "Back in a minute."

It was more like five minutes before she returned. "What can I get you?"

Dismissing the menu, Cami said, "Can I get two poached eggs and plain wheat toast? With cranberry juice?"

The waitress blinked. "We've got fried eggs and scrambled eggs."

Cami's shoulders slumped. "Scrambled. Do you have wheat toast?"

"Yeah. We got wheat toast. All out of cranberry juice. We've got orange and grapefruit."

"Fresh?" Cami asked hopefully.

The waitress looked at her like she was deliberately trying to cause trouble and simply shook her head.

"Grapefruit," Cami said.

Then the woman looked at Brand suspiciously. "You?"

"I'll have the three eggs over easy with bacon on the done side and waffle fries. Biscuits and gravy."

She smiled at him like he'd won a prize. "Coming right up."

When the waitress was gone, Cami said, "I think she likes you better than me."

"She's just jealous because you're cute."

She cocked her head to the side. "You rate girls for cuteness?"

"Sure. I've got eyes."

He loved the way she smiled like she really appreciated the compliment, like she didn't hear it nearly often enough. A woman like her ought to be told every single fucking day that she was everything to some lucky guy.

"So, navigator," he said, "how long do you figure it will take us to get to the Taylor County airfield?"

"If we keep the same pace as yesterday, four and a half hours." He nodded and glanced at his watch.

"Are we in a hurry?"

"Not exactly. I've just got a schedule in my head. I'd like to be there before three."

"Then maybe you shouldn't order enough breakfast to feed a football team at training camp." He laughed out loud. "And I should remind you that you're not working off all that fat and salt and carbs. Pretty soon the other boys are not going to think you're Adonis reincarnated."

When he trained his dark eyes on her they were twinkling like they were lit from within. "Sounds like you have a pretty high opinion of my body."

"Well, yeah. Doesn't everyone?"

Before he could answer, the waitress set a saucer-sized plate in front of Cami and two platters of food in front of Brandon. He picked up a piece of bacon, crunched down, and chuckled at Cami eyeing the amount of food in front of him.

"Growing boy," he said.

"No doubt. Don't come crying to me when you can no longer see your pretty toes."

He laughed. "You think my toes are pretty? I haven't

started the day with this many compliments… I don't know, maybe ever. You're taking a toll on my humility."

Cami found that she liked relaxed teasing Brandon a lot better than gruff bossy Brandon.

THE RAIN CONTINUED to pound all the way to Taylor County, Kentucky. In places they had to decelerate to a crawl because the water was covering the road. Luckily the SUV was high enough off the ground that they could pass without flooding so long as they went slow enough.

"Your guess was spot on. Four hours forty-five minutes," he said as they pulled into the parking area.

The airfield consisted of one strip long enough for small planes and two hangars. They ran for the side door and stood inside the threshold dripping on the concrete floor. There was a guy sitting in an office chair watching TV. He swiveled around to see who'd come in, but didn't look concerned. He looked a lot like what's left of Sammy Hagar.

"You Fornight?" he asked.

Brandon nodded. "Yeah. And you are?"

"Branch Copeland. I'll be your pilot today. Just sit back, relax, and leave the flying to me."

That sounded sarcastic enough to be alarming. Cami looked up at Brandon uncertainly.

"We'll see whether or not your flying deserves our relaxing. You ready to go?"

"Born ready." His eyes ran over Cami in a way that made Brandon's fists clench involuntarily. "You got luggage?"

"Yes."

"Bring it in the hangar. We need to see how much it weighs. You can drive in if you want."

Brandon leaned down to Cami and talked quietly. "You be okay here for a minute? While I get the car?"

She nodded. "Sure."

Brandon brought the car around and into the hangar where Copeland and Cami were waiting.

"Scales over there." Copeland pointed. "You first."

He waved at Cami, who drew back. "What do you mean, you first?"

"I mean get on the scale. The big guy is going to ride up front with me. After we establish your weight, I'll tell you how much of this," he nodded toward the luggage, "you can take."

She looked at Brandon. After he gave her a reassuring nod, she pressed her lips together and stomped toward the scale.

"A hundred and forty-three," said Copeland.

"I'm sure that's wrong," she said. "Your scale is faulty."

"Okay." He smiled without looking up. "Let's just say that your clothes weigh twenty-five pounds. Considering how wet you are, that may not be far off."

"Can we…?" Copeland looked up to see that her question was directed at Brandon. "Can we change before we leave? Put on dry clothes?"

"Absolutely." He turned to Copeland. "We'll change

and then weigh in."

"Fine with me," said the pilot. "Bathroom over there."

Cami unzipped one of her bags. "What's the weather like where we're going?"

Brandon fished out his phone, tapped around for a few seconds and then said, "It's cool. Fifties. Into forties tonight." He looked up at her with a big smile. "No rain."

She grinned and knelt down next to her open bag. She fished out dry skinny jeans with lots of give, an oversize turtleneck sweater, undergarments, boot socks and brown Frye riding boots. The combat-style boots she'd been wearing were wet on the inside and wouldn't be dry for a week.

She changed quickly and felt instantly better to be dry from the skin all the way out. She retrieved the garbage bag from where she'd left it in the office, stashed all the wet things in there, including the boots, then rifled through a different bag until she found a puffy vest.

"Okay. Done," she said, pulling the vest on.

"Climb up," Copeland said. She did. "One twenty-nine."

She smiled at Brand like she'd won a blue ribbon and he couldn't suppress a grin. *Women.*

"So you can take a hundred and thirty pounds of luggage between the two of you."

Cami looked at her three pieces. She had no idea what they weighed.

"While you're figuring that out, I'm changing," Brandon said, though it seemed like no one else was listening.

Cami zipped up both bags that she'd been into. She wheeled the first over and wrestled it up onto the scale, scowling at Copeland when he offered no help.

"Forty-eight pounds." He fed that into his calculator.

She pulled that bag off and repeated the process with the second rolling case.

"Forty-three pounds." He fed that into his calculator.

She put her shoulder strap soft side on last.

"Eighteen pounds. That leaves twenty-one pounds."

Brandon returned looking scrumptious in jeans, a heather gray Henley, and a pair of scuffed brown Ropers. He stuffed his wet clothes and boots into the garbage bag with Cami's things.

"You've got twenty-one pounds left," Copeland said.

Brandon put his athletic bag on the scale. There wasn't much left in it.

"Twenty-four pounds. You're over by three."

Brand unzipped the bag, pulled out his brown leather jacket, put it on, then set the bag back on the scale.

"Twenty pounds. Good to go," he announced and slid his phone into a vest pocket.

"You've already done flight check?" Brandon asked.

"Yep. We've got wind resistance from the north, but we should have plenty of fuel to get there without stopping. ETA is six o'clock."

"Good. We'll be there before dark. You got snacks?"

"This ain't Braniff first class," Copeland said.

Brandon gave him a look of warning. "No. It's not even Dogpatch economy, but that doesn't answer the question."

"I got a box of cookies. A couple of bananas."

"Bring them," Brandon said, making it clear to Copeland that an invisible line of acceptable behavior had been established.

Brand went back to the SUV to get the rest of their stash. They still had three bottled waters, six protein bars, and two apples. It wouldn't be lunch at Emiles, but it would do.

He helped Copeland strap the luggage into the seat next to Cami to balance the load the best way possible. When they were all in the plane and settled, Brandon said, "You are instrument rated, right?"

"Yeah. I'm not suicidal. I want to live. Just like you."

Brand blew out a breath. "Okay. Let's see what you've got."

"Gonna be a little bumpy."

"Understood." Brand did understand that. There was no way to fly through that storm without getting knocked around a little. He looked over his shoulder with a silent question for Cami. She was nodding when the engines roared to life.

CHAPTER EIGHT

New York

I T DIDN'T TAKE long for Richard to reach a decision. Opportunities like the one he'd been offered by Trey Michaels didn't come along often. Giving Michaels what he wanted certainly wasn't illegal. And it wasn't as if the man intended Cami any harm.

Richard had nothing against Cami. She'd always been decent to him. Like Trey had said, Richard could be the hero in the story of a marriage going through a rough patch.

He knew Cami was trying to lie low, out of pocket, until after the divorce. He didn't know why, but he believed that heiresses were often high strung and frequently overly dramatic.

He didn't want to play games and make Michaels wait for an answer. On the contrary, he wanted to nail the deal down before Michaels had a chance to change his mind. It wasn't as hard to find a pay phone as he'd thought. He supposed he just didn't notice them anymore, but they were still around. And at two minutes after nine, he was dialing the number he'd memorized.

"Just a minute," Michaels said. He got up and closed the door to his office. "Go ahead."

"I accept your terms."

"Excellent. What do you have for me?"

"I don't know where she is, but I do know that he hired a security service."

"Who?"

"Sanctuary Security. It's actually an offshoot business of a motorcycle club out of Austin, Texas."

"Motorcycle club? Huh."

"Sons of Sanctuary."

"Like Hell's Angels?"

"I only know what I've told you."

"Good work, Richard."

"If you learn more, call me at this number, but only at this number. Do you understand?"

"Yes, sir. When do you…?"

Michaels ended the call and dialed the best private investigator/hacker he knew.

"This is Dalli."

"Got work for you."

"Listening."

"I need to know everything you can find out about people associated with Sanctuary Security and the Sons of Sanctuary Motorcycle Club located in Austin, Texas."

"Okay."

"How long?"

"I can start on it in… just a minute, four days maybe."

"Now."

"Hold on, I'm…"

"Now. Whatever it takes."

"Whatever it takes?"

"Don't make me repeat myself. I need this information now and I'll triple your regular rate."

"Done."

"How long?"

"Three hours. Look for a courier."

"Alright. Send me an invoice."

"Yeah. Count on it."

BY LUNCHTIME TREY Michaels had made his office aware that he didn't want to be disturbed and was looking through a treasure trove of information that had arrived on a flash drive by courier. The ability to scan information and quickly isolate critical data was one of the talents that had helped him amass extraordinary wealth and stature while still relatively young.

While there was plenty about the SSMC that was interesting, and under other circumstances might have even been entertaining, he wasn't interested in the club or the security company. He was interested in the people. Starting with club members. If he didn't find what he was looking for there, he'd expand the search to wives, girlfriends, and other relatives of club members.

In that case it wouldn't be necessary to look at non-members. His uncanny ability to read people and identify weaknesses, even from afar and on paper, led him straight to what he was looking for.

Edgar Raymond Stiles.

Known by Sons of Sanctuary club members as 'Edge'.

Looking at his history, Michaels could see that, over the years, club members had done well for themselves with ever increasing personal assets and responsibilities. Except for Edge.

He'd been working at Hollywood Wrecks and Rides, mostly answering phones so far as Michaels could tell, since he was nineteen. He made fifty thousand dollars a year, which was a fraction of what other club members were pulling in. He suspected that Stiles knew he'd been passed over for pretty much everything, which meant that there was almost certainly underlying resentment festering and quietly waiting for someone like Michaels to recognize and exploit.

He pressed a button near his right hand. Within seconds an assistant opened the door.

"Yes, sir?"

"Get Razenach."

"Yes, sir."

CHAPTER NINE

Austin, Texas

Edgar Raymond Stiles, known by SSMC club members as Edge, thought of himself as being unlucky. Even though he'd been loyal to the club and had never talked against management, he hadn't been lucky enough to land one of the plum jobs that resulted in major scratch. At best, he felt overlooked. At worst, he felt ignored.

He'd been with the club since he was nineteen years old. He stole a car and got caught, but his dad, who wasn't rich, bought him a community service sentence. Brant had known Edge's dad since the days when Brant was head mechanic at the Yellow Rose. Edge's dad had worked for Brant for a while before moving on and eventually opening his own German auto repair.

Reading the signs of more trouble to come, Edge was sent to Brant to straighten him out. Brant put him to work as a prospect and figured he'd spoil out in a couple of weeks. He didn't. Edge did any and every job he was given, no matter how monotonous, ridiculous, or demeaning. And he did it without complaining. While that was to his credit, the other club members would have had to struggle to find something else nice to say.

Because there wasn't an apparent reason to dislike Edge and kick him out, everybody let him slide, secretly thinking that the problem with him must be their own issue.

So year after year, Edge answered phones at the Hollywood Wreck and Ride and flew under the club radar.

If asked, he would have said that he was just as unlucky with women. He studied the way other club members interacted with the ladies. He tried to mimic what they said, what they did, but instead of getting him an invitation to a bed, or even a parking lot, he got the cold shoulder.

Women seemed to recoil when he came near. He wasn't gorgeous like Arnold, but he wasn't bad-looking either. At least he didn't think so. Didn't matter though. He knew when he wanted to get it wet, he was going to have to pay. And because he'd come to think of the fairer sex as wicked withholders of what he wanted and needed, he paid extra for the privilege of meting out punishment.

It had been a while, which was why he was watching a double stuff porn on his laptop when Razenach walked into the showroom. Razenach didn't know that because Edge had the sound muted and was sitting behind a mahogany reception console.

Normally Edge would have gotten up and gone to greet the customer, as he'd been taught to do, but he had a bit of a chubby. So he decided to stay put until he got that under control.

"Welcome to Hollywood Wreck and Ride," he said without getting up.

When the man turned his gaze toward the greeter, Edge's halfie went limp quick. The guy looked like a preppie throwback. He was wearing a pale gray Polo tee with color, the kind with the hem shorter in the front than in the back, untucked over Levi's. The Sperry topsiders completed the look.

If it wasn't for what Edge saw behind those blue eyes, he would have taken the guy for more money than sense.

Edge got up and approached the man with the wariness usually reserved for rattlesnakes.

"What can we do for you?"

"Edgar Raymond Stiles?" The hair stood up on the back of his neck, but Edge managed to nod. "I'm Mr. Razenach. I'd like to outline a proposal that I believe you'll find attractive."

Edge poured coffee from the showroom set up and sat down to listen to what the man had to say.

CHAPTER TEN

New Mexico

TRUE TO EXPECTATION, the flight was rough for the first forty-five minutes, but gradually became smoother until they flew out of the rain pattern. The dark clouds became lighter clouds and finally see-through mists before they broke into bright sun and clear blue sky.

They were flying low enough to see everything below. Cami watched the ground as they flew over the forests and lakes of Arkansas, the Red River, the desolate plains of West Texas, into buffalo country in New Mexico.

"You know," said the pilot, "a lot of people don't know it, but when the pioneers came through here this country was covered with grass high as a horse's knees. The Indians burned the forests every now and then to keep the buffalo plentiful. And so they could see who was comin'.

"All this is the result of overgrazing a century before there was any understanding of land management. Thing is, once this happens, you can't just snap your fingers and bring it back. Rain clouds drift over vegetation and drop rain where stuff is growing. If you take the vegetation, you invite desert. Permanently."

"I didn't know that," Brandon said.

"That's us." Copeland pointed at an airstrip ahead. Within minutes they were on the ground with one of the smoothest landings Brandon had ever experienced. He certainly couldn't have matched it himself.

They taxied to the hangar which sat about thirty yards away from the house, which was an enormous sprawling one story stucco complex with Monterey tiles on the roof. There was no doubt in Cami's mind that the owner had some scratch.

The pilot pulled the plane up to the fuel station and shut down the propellers.

By the time Brandon had helped Cami down from the plane, the owner had walked over.

He extended his hand to Brand. "I'm Knox," the man said. He looked to be about the same age as Brant, in other words, old enough to be Brandon's father. He'd kept himself in decent shape and had probably been a heartbreaker in his twenties.

"Brandon Fornight." He shook Knox's hand.

Knox laughed softly. "You didn't need to tell me that. You look a whole hell of a lot like your dad."

Brandon put his hand on the small of Cami's back, a possessive gesture that Knox registered immediately.

"Nice to meet you, young lady."

Cami smiled. "You have a beautiful place here, Mr. Knox."

"Just Knox. Come on inside." He motioned to a man they hadn't noticed before. "Alberto. Bring the luggage inside."

"Oh we're not staying," Brand said. "My dad said there'd be a car."

"There is. But it'll be dark in four hours. Stay for the night. Got lots of room and you can get started in the morning."

"I really appreciate the offer, Knox, and believe me, it's tempting, but we need to get on the road."

Brand didn't want to give the real reason for declining the offer. The truth was that Brandon felt like he'd be endangering Knox and his people on the ranch. Knox had done a favor for his dad and for the SSMC, by letting them land there, but that was where it should end.

Knox smiled and nodded. "Well, another time maybe." When Knox waved at something behind him, Brandon turned to see who or what it was. "Alberto. Bring that car." The man lifted his hand in acknowledgement.

Raising his voice so that Copeland could hear him, Knox said, "Same for you. If you want to stay over, we got room and dinner."

"Sounds good," Copeland said.

"You need anything else?" Knox turned back to Brandon.

"I think we're good," Brand said.

"Well, hope you brought short sleeves. We've got a warm front coming up from the south this evening."

Brand looked at Cami. The idea of a 'warm front' was clearly to her liking.

"After two days of being wet, sometimes wet *and* cold, warm and dry sounds good."

Knox chuckled. "And it's free if you're in the right place at the right time."

"Truer words were never spoken."

They turned when Alberto stopped the car next to the plane where Copeland was unloading luggage. He hopped out and began transferring the bags to the trunk and rear seat of a car that looked like its better days were long gone. It was dented in places and missing plate in others.

"Don't judge a book by its cover," Knox said as if he was reading Brand's mind. "This is a new Hyundai with a V8 and a few enhancements that would thrill Mad Max." Brand and Cami shared a WTF glance. "It may look like a beater, but don't let that fool you. I hope you don't have to find out what she'll do, but if you need performance, don't worry. It'll be there." He looked at Cami. "Your old man must think a lot of you because this car cost him dearly."

She wasn't sure how to respond to that. So she smiled and said, "I'm sure I'm worth it?"

Knox laughed. "Sure you are, too, darlin'."

She went around to the driver's side.

"What are you doing?" Brand asked from beside her.

"It's my turn."

"Oh yeah?"

"Yeah."

"I'm rested. I'll take first shift."

For a minute he thought she might launch a protest. He could see the conflict on her face. But she sighed and walked around to the other side of the car.

Three and a half hours of little traffic and sparse scrub brush later, he was still driving. It seemed the concept of taking turns had escaped him.

As they pulled into Alamagordo, Cami said, "I'm hungry. Let's at least stop for dinner." Brandon's stomach agreed wholeheartedly. "Oh, look. Casa de Rosa. New Mexican food sounds great, doesn't it?"

"New Mexican food?"

"You've never been out of Texas before?" Brandon had to smirk at that. He'd probably logged as many international miles as the Secretary of State. "You thought TexMex was the beginning and end of enchiladas? Then you would be very wrong, my friend."

Without warning he did a U turn that would make a stunt man proud. He expected Cami to shriek or offer up some respectable expletives, but she giggled instead. He couldn't suppress the grin that resulted from hearing that sound and he wondered if she'd been a wild thing before Michaels.

"I'm going to eat until I look pregnant," she said.

"No, you won't. You'll nibble at lettuce and complain about fried tortilla chips."

She laughed that guttural throaty laugh that she saved for special occasions. He hadn't yet figured out the code of her various sounds of delight, but he was working on it.

"Not today. Today I'm eating melted cheese and guacamole."

"Guacamole doesn't count. It's healthy."

"Okay. Well I'm also eating meat. Lots of meat. And did I say cheese?"

"You might have mentioned it."

When he drove past the front door, around to the side, she said, "Wait! Where are you going?"

"Simmer down. Just checking things out."

He drove around the entire building before deciding to park in the back as he had for breakfast. When they got out of the car, they realized that the 'warm front' had arrived. It felt more like a summer day than a New Mexico dusk.

Brand tried the kitchen door and found it open. The kitchen staff looked up with open curiosity. In response, Cami smiled and he shrugged.

They claimed the booth closest to the kitchen door. Again, Brand positioned Cami with her back to the front door and put himself where he could see everything.

The hostess who said okay to them sitting away from all the activity gave them menus and left. After a couple of minutes of looking at the selection, Cami said, "I'm having fajitas al carbon."

"No. You can't have fajitas," Brandon said.

"Why not?"

"Because fajitas are not New Mexican."

"Sure they are."

Brand was shaking his head. "Nope. They were invented by Ninfa Laurenzo in Houston, Texas."

She narrowed her eyes. "How do you know that?"

"Every lover of Mexican food knows that," he said in an aggravatingly snobby way.

"Well, I'm sure they do them with a New Mexico flair here."

He chuckled. "You're *sure* of that, are you?"

A middle-aged man with gray hair, gray eyes, and a gray apron over jeans came up. "Evening. What can I get you?"

"Fajitas al carbon," Cami said.

"Beef or chicken?"

"Both?"

He nodded. "Flour or corn tortillas?"

"Corn."

"Will you have a margarita with that?"

She hadn't thought about it, but a margarita didn't sound half bad. "Well…"

"We have blackberry tonight. House special."

"Blackberry margarita?" He nodded. "Yes. I have to try that."

"You won't be sorry." He turned to Brandon. "You, sir?"

"I'll have the Governor's Deluxe Combo. No alcohol. Water's fine."

"Sure. So you folks here for the concert?"

Brandon opened his mouth to say no, but Cami beat

him to it with, "What concert?"

"It's the last one of the year. When the full moon shines on the white sand it's almost as light as day. You should go see for yourself. You know the *Night Before Christmas*? The moon on the breast of the new fallen snow gave a lustre of midday to objects below? Well, that's what it looks like."

When the man left, Brandon was already shaking his head before Cami had a chance to turn on the pleading expression. He saw it coming. He was just about to deliver a definitive, "Not a chance," when the proprietor returned with a flyer.

Reading from it, he said, "It's Texas singer/songwriter, Rudy Wood, performing with the Tularosa Basin Musicians Union. They bring Wood's songs to life with slide guitar, mandolin, banjo, and harmonica." With that he left the flyer on the table and was gone again.

"Brandon, it's country! We have to go."

"We're not going, Rose."

"Okay, forget the music. We have to see the full moon on the white sand, right? I mean, when are we ever going to get a chance to do that again?"

"Sometime when we're not running from a possibly psycho, potentially dangerous husband."

Her mood went instantly serious. "He's not my husband. The legal formality may still be in process, but he became my ex-husband the minute I discovered he was planning to kill me." She leaned forward a little. "For *money*."

"Okay. I get the distinction, but the fact remains. Have you forgotten what we're doing out here? We're running from your ex who, as you just said, wanted to *kill* you. For *money*."

"Don't you want to see the lustre of midday on objects below? Come on. Look at it this way. You'll be able to see *everything*. Let's go. If it seems like it's too dangerous, I'll go peaceably." He shouldn't have any trouble saying no, but that hopeful face was making it hard. "What are you afraid of? Nobody's going to do anything with a bunch of music lovers around watching."

She had a point. It seemed unlikely that somebody working for Michaels would make a move at a music concert. Unless it was a sniper. But sniping was the wild card that was impossible to plan for, which sort of made it a non-factor.

When the proprietor or manager or waiter returned with Cami's purple margarita, Brand said, "How many people usually go to these things?" He indicated the flyer.

"Oh. Might get as many as two hundred."

"Two hundred," Brandon deadpanned. When someone said the word concert, the image that sprang to mind wasn't one of *maybe* two hundred people.

The man nodded as he left.

Cami put her hands together like she was begging.

Christ. How did anybody ever say no to her?

"We'll go check it out. If it looks like it's not any more dangerous than…"

"Being in a restaurant?"

Brandon's mouth didn't smile, but his eyes gave away his amusement. "Yeah. That."

She chatted happily through dinner, which wasn't bad at all, and made yummy sounds whenever she sipped blackberry margarita through a straw. "You really should try this. It's incredible."

"You're not seriously recommending that when you know that the only thing standing between you and potential mayhem is me."

Ignoring that, she said, "I'm stuffed," and pushed the oval-shaped plate away as if to put an exclamation point on her announcement.

The fact that Brandon was vulnerable to her wishes charmed her. It had been a long time since she'd felt like she had that kind of power over a man, the kind of power that made someone care about whether or not a woman was pleased. And for the hundredth time in the past twenty-four hours she found herself wishing that he wasn't gay.

Sure. It made traveling together as strangers a lot more relaxed, but damn. She had no trouble picturing him in all sorts of compromising positions. Positions being the operative word.

When they left the Casa de Rosa, they turned south toward Alamagordo. On the southern outskirts Brandon pulled into a motel with a sign that said The Lost Saucer Inn. It was a rundown motel with about twenty rooms. Not the sort of place anyone would ever expect Carmichael's only daughter to be spending the night.

"What are we doing?" she asked.

"Getting a room. Come.'"

He opened his door and got out.

After getting out of the car, she said, "Don't give me commands like I'm a dog."

He smiled on the inside because, even though her mouth rebelled, she followed. As he held the door open for her, he scanned for any suspicious activity. There was none. They were acting out a good plan and he knew it.

The Camden Carmichael he'd first seen in that New Jersey warehouse was beautiful. And this Camden Carmichael was beautiful, but you'd have to be close and know her pretty well to realize they were the same person.

Between the drastic change in looks and the drastic change in geography, it was unlikely she'd be found. But it was Brand's job to be vigilant regardless.

"Need a room for the night," he said to the clerk.

"Alright. You here for the concert?"

"That's right," said Brandon. "I'm a country music lover, how about you?"

He heard Cami snigger behind him as he smiled at the manager.

"Not so much," said the kid, "but full moon on the sand is kinda cool."

"Can't wait," Brand said as he retrieved his fake drivers' license and the credit card account opened in the same name. Bradley Forrester. "Thank you."

"Mr. Forrester?" Brandon turned around. Thank

goodness he'd chosen a name similar to Fornight. The clerk was holding out the key. "You forgot the key."

"Oh sure. Excited about tonight I guess."

The kid smiled. "Number forty-three."

"Forty-three? I don't see that many rooms."

The clerk rolled his eyes. "I know. The owner's into numerology. She has her own reasons for how and why the rooms are numbered."

"Okay." Brand lifted an eyebrow in solidarity with the kid's misgivings.

"Stop it," Cami said, looking between them. "That's as good a reason for numbering things as sequential order. Maybe she knows something we don't know."

"Look. Everybody's entitled to her own opinion, but does it look like she knows something we don't know?" The kid gave a small wave to indicate the condition of the establishment that cut his paycheck.

Cami lifted her chin. "I'm glad to have a warm, dry, clean place to spend the night." After a couple of seconds, she added, "The room is clean, isn't it?"

The kid grinned. "That is about the only good thing you can say. The owner is a maniac about clean. It's like that disorder where people can't stop cleaning."

"Obsessive compulsive?" Cami asked.

"Yes. Like that."

"Well, I hope it's not debilitating for her, but..." she looked at Brandon, "good for us?"

Brand held the key up. "Thanks again."

"Oh. About getting there tonight." He pointed to the

road outside. "Take 70 south. You'll run right into the park visitors' center. They'll give you directions. A lot of people bring folding chairs. But you can sit on the ground if you don't have them. I mean, the sand sort of conforms to your, um, body."

Brandon chuckled. "We don't have chairs with us, but we're both okay with conformity."

As they were leaving, she said, "Speak for yourself."

He chuckled. Handing her the key, he said, "You can check out the room while I bring in the stuff."

When he pulled up to number forty-three, she was out of the car as soon as it stopped rolling.

He grabbed the bags out of the back seat first and hauled them inside.

"A double bed," he said.

She turned and looked at the bed. "Is that a problem?"

He assumed her question meant that he'd said that out loud.

Yes. Yes it is.

"No. Why would it be?"

He turned without elaborating to retrieve the rest of the luggage.

"Come on," she said. "It's almost dark. We're going to miss it."

"We're not going to miss as much as I'd like to." She rolled her eyes. "I just need to sort through a few things."

She watched him hide various-sized guns. Two in a hunter-style vest with zippered pockets. One in a boot.

"Aren't you afraid of shooting yourself in the foot?"

"Metaphorically, yes. Physically, no."

"I'm bringing waters. We didn't ask if they sell stuff."

"They've probably got hot dog and pretzel stands."

"Ugh," she said in disgust.

"And tee shirts."

"Tee shirts?" She sounded as hopeful as a kid who's never been to an amusement park. "I want a tee shirt."

"You sound like you've never bought a souvenir tee shirt."

"I haven't."

He stared at her for a few seconds. "Okay. If they have tee shirts for sale, we'll get you one."

The grin she gave him made his heart melt into an ooey gooey mass of inexperience. Brandon had never been in love. He'd never even wanted to spend time with a woman outside the bedroom. He didn't want to put a name on what he was feeling because that would be too scary.

"I can't help but wonder what other kinds of great American experience you've missed," he said as he opened the door. When they were in the car and going south on 70, he said, "Have you ever been to an amusement park?"

"You mean like Disneyworld?"

"Yes. For example."

"No.

He nodded. "Have you ever been to a music festival? The kind that could fill up Central Park?"

"No."

"Have you ever been to the movies on a date?"

"Movies? Um, no."

He could see that she was beginning to wilt. Like his questions were making her feel like she'd missed out, and seeing her become smaller wasn't fun. So he decided to reverse that process.

"But I'll bet you've sipped brandy on a yacht underneath the palace at Monaco."

She smiled. "It was cognac and I wasn't drinking age. So it was an occasion."

"I'll bet you could jump horses in equestrian competition by the time you were twelve."

She laughed. "Yes."

"I'll bet you could tell me the difference between champagne powder in the Rockies and the kind of snow they get on the slopes in Lucerne."

She nodded. "That's right."

He looked over at her. "The world is full of millions of people who have tee shirts and crap from Disneyworld who would give anything for those experiences."

She took in a deep breath and turned to look out the window. Brandon wasn't just a centerfold in the flesh. He was a good guy. A kind person who went out of his way to make her feel good about herself. She hoped they'd be friends after she was no longer a job. Aside from the whole sexually-off-limits thing, he was special.

"When this is over," he said, "what are you hoping for? More than anything else?"

She was quiet for a few seconds before quietly saying, "To never be afraid again."

His heart clenched like a vise in his chest. By God, that's what he wanted for her, too.

They bought tickets at the visitors' center and were directed to parking.

Brandon had to admit it was a thing worth doing. It was bright as the full moon on new snow, but warm enough to be comfortable without a jacket. Some people were even wearing shorts. Although the sand reflected the light, the darkness in between gave the people some anonymity. Enough that he could relax.

He kept a watchful eye, but felt they were at least as safe as they'd been stopping for dinner in town. Maybe more.

Motel kid was right. The sand was soft enough to re-shape itself around any butt pressed against it. As for the music, he'd never tell Cami, but he was gradually accepting that some of it wasn't that bad.

Every now and then, he would forget what he was supposed to be doing and fall into the spell of a magical evening. Sitting next to a spikey-haired blonde on the white sands of an ex-missile testing site, listening to country music under a full moon seemed like the most natural thing in the world.

FOR THE SECOND day in a row, he woke facing a motel door with a warm and pliant body plastered to his back like she'd been superglued. Feeling her braless breasts crushed against him had his hand reaching down to brush morning wood. It wouldn't take much to get him off, but he didn't really want to take the risk. In his head he ran through the humiliation of having to explain. "Oh, sorry, did my jerking off wake you?"

He eased out of bed, went to the window, and pulled the curtain back far enough to check the parking lot. It was still dark, but would be light soon. Everything looked quiet.

He'd checked the map before going to bed and settled on a route. He figured there was less mountain driving if they went south toward El Paso, but cut west at 506 to head for Austin via Carlsbad, long before they came anywhere near the interstate. There was sparse population out there, which made it safer for Cami. He figured they could make it to Austin in ten hours.

He felt a little surge of excitement about getting home and about getting Cami home safely. But in order to make that happen, he had to get her up.

Grabbing his pillow, he threw it at her head, but maybe not quite as forcefully as the first time.

"Rise and shine," he said, scratching his balls on the way to the bathroom.

Her only answer was a groan.

"You can have the shower in three minutes if you want it. We're out of here in fifteen."

She sat up looking tousled, sleepy, and... adorable, until she started yelling. "Fifteen minutes! I can't shower and get ready to go in fifteen minutes. Even suggesting that is barbaric."

"One person's barbarian is another person's body-guard."

"Witty, Brandon. Comedians are supposed to come out at night."

"Two minutes."

"Ugh!"

While she was in the shower, Brandon called his dad to check in and let him know the situation.

"We'll be there by dinner so you need to have a place ready for Ms. Carmichael."

"Ms. Carmichael? Jesus, Brand. You haven't let the girl out of arm's reach for two days and you're not on a first name basis?" The pause spoke volumes to Brandon's dad. "Jesus Christ, Brandon. Did I really need to say that clients' daughters are off limits?"

"I haven't touched her."

"Okay then. My bad. Read that wrong, I guess."

Edge emerged from his room at the club. He walked by Brant's office on his way to the kitchen to get break-fast. Brash was leaning against the door jamb.

"They left Alamagordo. He says they'll be back to-night by supper. They're headed toward El Paso, but cutting off at 506 to Carlsbad."

"That's close to…"

"Yeah," Brant said. "I'll breathe a lot easier once we get your brother back here. I've been uneasy about giving him this job. I love him, but he's a paper pusher. Not ex special ops."

"Maybe not, but he's resourceful. It's in his blood."

"Not a time for self-congratulations, Brash. I haven't slept a wink. Haven't told your mother either. I don't like hiding things from her, but I suspect I'd get an earful if she knew what he was doing."

Edge eased behind Brash so quietly he never knew he was there.

"WE HAVE TO go to the McDonalds for breakfast and get those things you told me about!"

"Do you have to go to the bathroom?"

"No. Why?"

"Because, if you don't have to go to the bathroom, we're going to use the drive through."

"Drive through," she repeated, sounding inappropriately excited. "Wait. Pull over and let me drive. If we're going to do drive through, I want to drive."

He glanced at her incredulously. "You've never been through drive through."

She shook her head.

"Okay. We might as well top off the tank."

He pulled into a gas station close to McDonalds. "While we're here, I might as well go to the bathroom and restock our snack supply."

Brandon opened his mouth to say something about doing a one eighty on restroom usage, but thought better of it. Instead he went with, "*Our* snack supply? You're a quick study, Rose. Alright, but wait until I'm done here."

When he returned the nozzle to its holder and

screwed the gas cap back on, Cami got out. After he checked it out, she used the toilet, whether she needed to or not, then gathered up bottled waters, bananas, nuts, and protein bars.

"Get juice to have with breakfast in the car."

Back in the car, she was excited about her first drive through experience and excited to be the driver driving through the drive through.

"Just ease up to that lighted sign. There's a speaker for talking to the people inside."

When she was in position, a voice said, "Ready for breakfast when you are."

She looked at Brandon and mouthed, "What do I say?"

He chuckled. "Three Egg McMuffins." She repeated that. "Two hashbrowns." She repeated that.

"Drive to the first window."

She grinned at Brandon before pulling up to the first window. He handed her some bills, which she passed on to the lady waiting for payment.

"Put the change in the box," Brandon said.

"The box?"

"Yeah. That plastic thing under the window."

She read the box. "A charitable bodyguard."

"Don't go thinking I'm soft, Rose. I'm passing that on to your dad."

She drew in a big breath and nodded.

Once they were out of town, on the road again, Brandon peeled the paper away from her round sandwich and handed it to her.

"You want cranberry juice?"

"Yes."

He fished the cranberry out of the convenience store sack, opened it, and set it in the drink holder next to her right arm. It was a thoughtful thing to do. She tried to remember if Trey had ever been thoughtful like that, even before they were married, when he was actually *trying* to impress her. Maybe he had. So much had happened since then it was hard to remember.

"Well, what do you think?" Brandon asked with his mouth full.

She smiled while chewing, glanced his way, and nodded. When she swallowed, she said, "Yeah. Good. That's three new experiences this morning."

"Okay. There's the drive through."

"Yes."

"And the McMuffin."

"Yes."

"What's the third?"

"The third is a secret."

"Come on."

"Lips are sealed."

"Two can play that game. I had an experience this morning I've never had before, too."

"What?"

"Not telling," he said as he took a bite of hash browns.

"You're lying."

"Definitely not lying."

"That's not fair."

He laughed. "It's so fair the goddess Justice is grinning ear to ear."

She huffed. "Still not telling."

"Fine with me, but I'll just say this. Fantasizing about gay guys is futile."

He switched on the radio and located a rock station.

"Nobody said my third new experience had anything to do with you, Brandon! And I'm driving so I should get to choose the music."

He laughed at her again. "You think you should get to choose the music when it's your turn to drive and when it's my turn to drive. You're a radio hog. Plus, you lost a turn because of last night."

She gaped. "Last night?"

"I listened to two hours of country music."

"That doesn't count."

"It does." He turned the volume up louder and sat back looking satisfied and smug.

Half an hour south of Alamagordo, on a stretch of road with no cars in sight, Brandon was singing along to some Pulled Pork song at the top of his lungs when Cami reached over and turned off the radio.

He opened his mouth to protest, but stopped.

"Is that a helicopter?" she asked.

Brand could hear it above, way too close, but couldn't see it, which meant it had to be directly overhead and keeping pace with the car.

"Yeah, it is," he said. A quick glance at Cami told him

she was terrified. "Don't be scared, Rose. We've got this covered."

She looked over at him and nodded, but didn't look any less frightened.

He pulled the burner phone out of his vest pocket and punched in his dad's *other* phone number. The one used for security communications on this one job. The one that was supposed to become obsolete within a few hours.

"What's wrong?" Brant answered.

"We're thirty miles south of Alamagordo and we've got a helicopter trying to land on the roof of the car."

"Keep going and don't stop. I'll get you some back up, but it may take twenty minutes."

"What do you mean?"

"That car is capable of everything a car can do. Try to drive your way out of this. If you can't, if that thing tries to land close to you, shoot the gas tank and get the hell away."

Brandon swallowed, his mind racing. "Okay."

"Keep the phone handy."

"Okay."

The call went dead.

There was just one problem. He couldn't 'drive his way out of it' because Cami was behind the wheel. And they couldn't exactly stop on the side of the road and change drivers. He'd been an idiot agreeing to let her behind the wheel and now they were going to pay for that mistake.

Brandon tried to remember if he'd ever felt fear before. Maybe he had, but nothing like the needle pricks of adrenaline running through his system. His molars pressed against each other as he grappled with getting his emotions under control and he realized, like a lightning bolt epiphany, that his fear was for Cami's safety, not his own.

He steadied his voice before he spoke.

"Help is coming. We just have to keep driving."

"Help? What kind of help?"

"Back up. That's all I know, but I trust my old man."

"Your old man? You mean your father?"

"Yes. He owns Sanctuary Security."

"Oh."

"Just keep driving. Don't speed up. Don't slow down."

She nodded a little too fast and he knew, without checking her pulse, that her heart was pounding.

"If they get me…"

"They're not going to get you, Rose."

Brandon unbuckled his seat belt and hauled the duffel with the weapons to the floor board behind them and unzipped it. He set two pistols in the drink holder console after checking to make sure they were loaded. He hadn't brought a rifle. When choosing what weapons might be needed on this sort of assignment, shooting the gas tank of a helicopter wasn't a scenario that had come to mind.

He pulled out the Smith and Wesson 657 Varminter six shooter. It was made for prairie dogs and their kin, but it was the closest thing to ideal in his bag of goodies.

The Varminter had a red dot optic for closer range, which meant that even if fear had him at a disadvantage, he'd know where his shot was going before he fired. If the target exceeded the optic range, there was also a Bushnell Scope that could get him accuracy up to a hundred yards. Either way, he wasn't going to be able to set up a tripod and take his time like he was a weekend enthusiast at the gun range.

Brandon had loaded the sixth bullet when the helicopter swooped down in front of the car. He heard Cami's sharp intake of breath, but she didn't shriek or scream or react like women in the movies. She shook from trembling, but managed to keep her hands steady on the wheel as she jerked the vehicle to the left. A lot of vehicles would have responded to that maneuver by rolling off into the ditch, but the Hyundai kept all four tires on the road.

"Good girl. Don't worry, Rose. You're not going with them. No matter what."

She glanced over at Brandon as if to try to discern the honesty of that pronouncement. Her brows were drawn together and her hands were still shaking. She seemed to find the reassurance she was seeking in Brandon's expression because, after that, she calmed. Visibly.

"No matter what," she repeated.

The way she said that told Brandon that her years with Michaels had been even worse than she'd described.

The incident lasted no longer than two seconds, but

the copter made it clear that they were bored with keeping pace and eager to start a cat and mouse game. All of a sudden the deafening propeller noise faded.

An eighteen-wheeler was coming toward them on the other side of the road, about a mile away. Apparently whatever the occupants of the helicopter planned, they didn't want witnesses. They did a fast ascent to keep from being identified.

He glanced at the map. They were only twenty-five minutes from the next town. If he could get them to a place with witnesses all around, they had a good chance of waiting out his pop's 'back up', whatever that was. Brandon knew his father had resources. Hell. For all he knew the old man was going to scramble jet fighters and sick them on the copter that was at a distance but still audible.

"Pull over. Fast as you can without killing us. And trade places with me."

She hit the brakes, shoved the car into park, and was out running around in less than a minute. Brandon had to admire the efficiency with which she executed his request.

Brandon was going nearly eighty miles per hour by the time he was fastening his seat belt. When the truck was out of sight, they heard the noise of the rotating helicopter blades getting louder. Brandon was pushing the car toward one twenty, but it was a straight flat stretch of road, safer than any race track. Still, Cami's knuckles were white where she was holding on.

The helicopter made a sudden dip. Brandon stomped on the brakes which caused the car to burn rubber and fish tail. Cami let out a small sound, but Brand could hardly hold that against her. Under the circumstances she was practically cool and composed.

The pilot and the guy next to him were close enough that Brandon and Cami could see their faces.

"Hold on," he said, before slamming the car into reverse and executing an inverted three point turn.

For a brief time they were headed the other direction. As fast as they were going, they caught up with the eighteen wheeler they'd passed. They rode his tail for ten minutes until he slowed and turned off at a ranch.

"Christ. Just our luck. It's a cattle truck."

Since the helicopter was out of sight and audibly absent as well, Brandon made a U turn so that they were heading south again. He was still spooked enough to want to get to civilization fast so he put the accelerator to the floor.

Why had he thought sparse population was such a great idea? What they needed was witnesses. Lots of them. And all they had was a mesa with grama grass, cactus, and a nice view of mountains in the distance.

They'd been speeding south for ten minutes. Just before hearing the helicopter, Brandon had been starting to feel hopeful that their pursuers had given it up. The copter practically dove at them.

Brandon had to pull a hard right to keep from running into them and, though the people in the helicopter might have been ready to commit hara-kiri, he was not. He'd just figured out that he had a lot to live for.

It looked like he'd successfully avoided the copter, but a rear tire caught loose gravel and sent the car rolling so that it was upside down. They were both hanging from seatbelts.

"You okay?" he asked her.

"Brandon. Don't let them…"

He fought with the buckle holding him prisoner until it gave way and dropped him on his head. He was trying to lay hands on one of the guns, when he heard a man's voice yell, "You want her out of there?"

"No! This couldn't have worked out better. Just set fire to the car and we're done. Perfect accident."

Cami heard it, too. Her gaze found Brandon's and held on like she was saying goodbye. And something else.

Their eyes were thus locked together when they heard the sound of salvation. A roar mightier than a dozen whirling rotary blades.

Engines were shut off by the time Brandon finally laid hand on one of the pistols. He pushed the door open and crawled out to find twenty guys wearing colors, holding guns on the three guys who were in the helicopter. One of the new arrivals, with gray-streaked black hair, walked over, reached inside the helicopter, and cut the engine like he knew what he was doing.

"You all right?" he asked Brandon. Brand nodded as his eyes flicked to the PRESIDENT patch on the man's cut. "Your pop sent us to make sure you found your way out of this fix. Go way back, your dad and me. Name's Axel."

"I need to get…"

"Ow!"

Axel grinned in an engaging way that would never suggest his men were disarming the three guys at gunpoint and forcing them to their knees, execution style, which seemed kind of risky since it was a public highway in bright morning sunlight. "Sounds like she figured out how to get loose herself."

There were a few quiet chuckles in response to the president's observation.

Brand looked around. They were wearing Dust Devils patches. Since Brandon hadn't grown up in club life, he had no idea who was who in terms of Texas motorcycle clubs.

Cami made her way around to Brandon's side. He looked down at her and it was all he could do not to put his arm around her and drag her into his side to show her and everybody else that she was protected. And his.

Axel waved to a couple of guys. "Get their stuff outta that car. We need to get outta here." To Brand he said, "What do you want to do with them?"

"You got a ride for us?"

Axel looked over just as four men had rocked the Hyundai back upright. One of them got in and turned the ignition. The V8 came to life. The guy in the driver's seat said, "We got action."

"Charlie. Drive that thing back. Brandon and his lady'll take your ride." He looked down at Cami. "Assumin' she's ridin' with you?"

Brand leveled a look at Axel. "Yeah. She's with me." He looked over at the guys on their knees. "Wait here," he told Cami. He walked over to the car and hunted around until he found the Varminter then walked back to Axel. "Go ahead and take off with the car. The helicopter won't be following today."

Axel took his meaning and nodded.

Brandon walked over to Charlie's ride and swung a leg over. He motioned for Cami, but she shook her head no. "No? What do you mean no?"

"I mean no. I'm not getting on that thing. They scare me."

There was a chorus of guffaws at that as Dust Devils mounted their bikes one by one.

"After what you've just been through, riding on a motorcycle scares you?" She nodded, looking small, vulnerable, and a little lost. "You know how we're working on never being scared again?" She didn't respond, but simply watched him like he held the key to all wisdom. He reached out, encircled her wrist with one big hand, and gently pulled her toward him. "We're working on it together. But we have to meet the fear halfway."

For a second she thought she saw something in the way he was looking at her, something that looked a lot like desire. A woman knows when a man is about to grab her and kiss her senseless. That was exactly what her heart and her body were telling her, but her brain was reminding her that it couldn't be that.

Probably wishful thinking.

He watched her take in a big breath that made her chest heave just before she got on behind him. It wasn't a small thing. Her actions were saying that she trusted him with her life.

Brandon fired up Charlie's bike and trained the long barrel of the Smith and Wesson on the three guys still on their knees. When Charlie pulled away, Brandon said, "I strongly suggest you guys start running unless you want to be the gooey part of s'mores." The three of them looked at each other for less than a heartbeat before they got to their feet and started running away from the road. "Tell Michaels if he comes for this woman again, he's going to be hunted by the Sons of Sanctuary," he shouted.

He turned the bike around in the road and went fifty yards before he stopped, used his forearm to steady the Varminter, and fired. He hit the gas tank in one shot and the explosion was probably heard for miles.

Cami was holding on to Brand tight as they flew down the road and fell in with the Dust Devils. Since she'd spent the past two nights plastered to his back, being pressed against Brandon was as familiar as his smell and the feel of his hard body. She rested her cheek against a shoulder blade and sighed, believing that the worst was over.

They followed the Dust Devils to a complex just east of El Paso where there wasn't much to speak of except… dust. There were several buildings including a large warehouse. The doors opened almost by magic as they approached. Brandon backed Charlie's bike into the line by the south wall and shut it down.

The two prospects at the bay doors didn't close them until the Hyundai was inside followed by one other biker.

He was a big redheaded guy, in his early forties maybe. He walked over to where Axel was dismounting. Axel grinned and clasped his hand in a gesture of greeting and affection. They exchanged a few words and then the guy turned and grinned at Brand. The interesting thing about him, at least one of the interesting things, was that he was wearing SSMC colors. Except the bottom rocker didn't say Austin, Texas. It said NOMAD.

He walked over and offered his hand to Brandon. "Cannon Johns," he said simply.

Axel ended the phone call he was on and sauntered over wearing a grin that revealed the good looks of somebody who'd more than likely been a player in his day.

"Yeah, he's one of yours, but he's a friend to Dust Devils."

"I see that," Brand said.

"Just got off the phone with Brant. We have a plan. Come on over to the house and we'll talk about it."

CHAPTER ELEVEN

Texas

"WHAT'S THAT?" EDGE said as he slid onto a bar stool at the SSMC.

Rita shrugged. Some kind of crash.

The big screen TV over the bar was on the news. Apparently a helicopter had gone down somewhere near the Texas-New Mexico border, but there was no sign of passengers. Local firefighters put out the blaze.

A truck driver was being interviewed. "Yeah. I saw the smoke a long time before I could make out what it was. Strangest thing. It looks like it crashed right here on the highway and exploded or something, but there was nobody around."

Edge caught the look that passed between Brash and Brant. "Give me a beer," he said.

Rita opened a long neck wordlessly and pushed it over.

Edge took the brew and walked down the hall to his room. He closed and locked the door before opening his third dresser drawer to look for a designated phone under socks and boxers.

A simple text message was waiting.

Call.

Cannon Johns, Brandon, Cami, and Axel sat around Axel's kitchen table while his wife rushed around whipping up some tacos.

"Your pop says you were planning on getting back tonight." Brandon nodded. "Could be that's still gonna happen. Here's the plan."

"THAT MAY BE the best food I've ever eaten," Cami told Axel's wife, Marguerite, who flushed with pleasure. "I mean, *ever.*"

"Glad you liked it," she said, as she took the rest of the plates away.

Axel pulled his phone out of his pants and said, "Yeah?"

He listened and made a couple of 'hmm' responses, then said, "Okay," and shut his phone. He looked around the table. "Just make yourself at home and relax. Watch TV. Help yourself to the refrigerator. If you want to nap, or whatever, Marguerite will show you to the guest room. I'll be back to get you when it gets dark."

When Brandon turned on the TV and sprawled out on the couch, Cami nestled in beside him like she needed the comfort of his nearness. And nothing could have pleased him more. He was becoming addicted to having the woman close by.

Knowing they were safe and that he could relax fully,

Brandon was asleep within fifteen minutes. He slept all afternoon in that position, half sitting, half lying back.

Axel came through the kitchen door and stomped his boots. When he appeared in the living room, Cami nudged Brandon awake.

"He's back," she said so quietly it was almost a whisper.

Brandon sat up, scrubbed a palm down his face and looked over at Axel.

"You ready?"

"I don't know," Brand said. "We haven't heard the plan."

"Come on. I'll tell you while we walk over to the warehouse." He gave Marguerite a kiss that was borderline embarrassing.

"Hey," Johns said. "Let's get this done then you two can get a room."

Axel slapped her on the fanny and walked away chuckling. "That's exactly what I had in mind."

On the way over to the warehouse, Axel shared the details. "My boys have been out renting some vans while your pop was making the other travel arrangements. Here's what we're going to do."

TEN MINUTES LATER Brand, Cami, and luggage were in a black van being driven by Cannon Johns. There were three other identical black vans being driven by other club members that left at the same time. At the first major crossroads, the four vans went four different directions.

Brandon was in the front passenger seat. He asked Johns, "Have you been to this place before?"

"I've been nearby. Don't think we'll have any trouble finding it."

"So. What does the NOMAD patch mean?"

"Means I've got one more job to do and then I'm comin' home. To stay."

"Home is?"

"Austin. God's country. At least it used to be before the roads turned into parking lots that look like L.A. at rush hour." He sighed and shrugged. "Can't change where you're from."

Brand thought about where he was from. New York. The "get a rope" TV commercial came to mind.

"Yeah. Can't be helped," he agreed.

They'd been headed west for a while, but turned north onto a dirt road outside Cornudas and drove for another couple of miles.

"Think you're in the clear," Johns said. "If anybody was following, we'd see their lights."

Brandon nodded as they turned into a ramshackle house with a hangar in the back. They kept going past the house and stopped at the hangar.

"Your pop says he bought a single engine barnstorm-er for cheap. You sure you can fly it home?"

"I got my pilot's license when I was fourteen. It shouldn't be a problem."

Cami looked at him with surprise, but said nothing.

The owner, who had apparently seen them coming,

slid open the hangar doors. The building was brightly lit inside.

Brandon walked around the plane inside then said, "What the hell is this?"

"This, my friend, is a 1969 super AG-CAT." He said it as proudly as if he was a new papa.

"This thing belongs in a museum."

The owner bristled at the offense. "She'll get you to the capitol of the Lone Star State and she'll do it with no stops and a full two hundred fifty miles to spare."

"Jesus," said Brand, but he took a good look around, performing his own version of flight check and maintenance.

He concluded that, as unsafe as it appeared on first look, it was sound enough to get them home. Like the guy said, it was a fairly short flight.

"What crops are you dusting around here anyway?" Brandon asked.

"Bought this property to retire on. My wife speaks Mexican and likes it over here. But I weren't ready to give her up. Got a good price though. It's time. She's all yours."

"I don't suppose you have a lighted runway?"

The man made sounds that were a mix of laughter and coughing. "I got flat ground." He pointed with his whole hand. "Go due east. Don't deviate. Get her up before fifteen hundred feet."

"Jesus."

The man shook his head. "You got a limited vocabulary, boy."

Brandon looked at Cami. He'd feel a lot better if the thing had two engines, but he suspected the old guy was right. The plane was in good enough shape.

"I'll ship your luggage to the clubhouse," Johns said.

Brandon nodded and looked at Cami. "Pull out enough stuff for overnight. Just what'll fit in your lap."

Cami didn't say anything, but looked at him with baleful eyes like she wanted to cling to the only things that were familiar to her. She held his stare for a couple of seconds before turning away to make decisions about what to take and what she hoped she'd see later.

Brandon got her up into the seat behind the pilot. He went over the flight plan. Luckily he knew where the little airport was. It was only twenty minutes from the clubhouse. It was actually a flying school, but they had a runway they could light for training purposes.

"You good?"

Cami nodded. He could see that she was far from good, but in less than two hours, the hardest part of this would be over. At least that was the plan.

They pointed the plane due east before starting the engine.

Cannon Johns stood in the darkness and watched the plane's tail lights gradually rise into the air and then disappear.

"Well. That's that," said the former owner of a vintage plane.

"Guess so," said Johns.

With that he got into the black van and drove away.

CHAPTER TWELVE

Austin, Texas

ONCE THEY WERE in the air, Cami realized that she wouldn't take anything for the experience of flying close to the ground in an old barnstorming plane on a moonlit night. It was wonderful, magical, and the random thought flitted across her mind that, if she died right then, she'd die happy. With only one regret. She would have loved to kiss Brandon on the mouth and know how it felt, even if he wouldn't be into it.

After the first hour the little towns they flew over came closer and closer together. She didn't know their names and couldn't imagine what they looked like in the daytime, but the twinkling lights looked welcoming at that altitude at that time of night. They didn't fly over any big towns and didn't see any other flying objects, identifiable or not.

When she realized that they were in a controlled descent, she wasn't welcoming the end of a very special ride. As the ground got closer and closer, she asked herself when would she ever fly across West Texas on a clear, warm night again with Brandon as her pilot and protector? The answer, which was never, made her sad.

When they landed at Bee Caves Flying School, there were three Sheriff's Department vehicles waiting for them. Cami threw her overnight bag to Brandon before accepting his help to get down.

Brandon pulled out his phone before going further and called Brant. "We're here."

"Good to know. See you soon."

They walked over to meet the guy who'd emerged from the hangar. "Tom Maker," he said. "Your car's ready and waiting." He pointed at the car parked a few steps away and handed Brand the keys.

"Thanks," Brandon said. "We appreciate it. I guess my dad owns this plane."

Tom laughed. "I've got to hand it to you. It took balls to fly that contraption."

"Don't scare the lady," Brand said.

"That doesn't scare me," Cami said. "I knew I was safe with him."

Brand's chest filled with emotion when he heard that and he knew the instant the words left her mouth that he wanted to always be that guy. The one she knew she was safe with.

"Turns out you were right," Tom said. "We'll sort out what to do with the plane. The Smithsonian maybe."

Brand smiled, put his arm around Cami in a possessive and heterosexual way, and guided her to the car.

It was a quarter mile to the gate of the flying school. When they got there, they found three Sheriff's Department vehicles blocking the exit.

One of the deputies walked over to the driver's side window. When Brandon rolled it down he said, "You Brand?"

"Yeah?"

"Well, seems like your daddy's concerned about your safety." He leaned down and tipped his hat to Cami. Eyes moving back to Brandon, he said, "When your daddy's concerned, my boss is concerned. So we're going to tag along and make sure you make it home without incident. I'm all about keeping the roads free of incidents. So we're going to give you a nice quiet inconspicuous escort home."

"Much obliged." It was a phrase Brandon had picked up after moving to Texas, a thing men said to each other that conveyed both thanks and respect. "Didn't catch your name."

The deputy smiled. "Names are for drinkin' buddies." He slapped the hood of the car and walked off toward his patrol SUV.

They followed the deputy and were followed by an additional two cars. When they reached the gates of the SSMC, they waited until Brandon and Cami were inside and then disappeared into the night.

One of the prospects closed the compound gates behind them.

"So this is where you live?" Cami asked.

"No. I have a place in town. A couple of the guys live here. Most have their own homes."

VICTORIA DANANN

"Oh." She hadn't confronted the possibility that she would be saying goodbye to Brandon when they reached the compound, and wasn't ready. "You're not staying here?"

He heard the anxiety in her voice. "You're as safe here as you would be if you were in a Fort Knox bunker."

Noting that he didn't answer the question, she looked at the buildings lit by outdoor halogens on poles. "I know, but I'm, um, used to *you*."

Brand opened his mouth to say something, but before he could, somebody opened the driver's side door.

"You gonna sit out here all night?"

It was Carlot. Brand got a half hug and slap on the back when he got out of the car. "Your pop has been a bear with a bee hive up his ass while you've been gone. We're all glad to see this over." He looked at Cami, who had gotten out of the car and was gripping her overnight bag in front of her like it was a lifesaver. "You did good."

It was Carlot's way of letting Brand know that he'd gotten what he wanted out of the gig. Respect from the club members.

"Thanks." He walked around to Cami and took her bag. "Carlot, this is Ro… This is Camden Carmichael." He put his arm around Cami again, something that was becoming a habit, and gave her a little squeeze. "Come on. Let's get you settled."

Carlot held open the door and they stepped inside the clubhouse. It was on the quiet side. Apparently Brant had read everybody the riot act about not scaring the client's

178

daughter.

The big screen TV was on above the bar. Three club members sat on stools with long necks. They looked Cami over and nodded at Brandon.

Brant emerged from the hallway that led to his office with a big grin on his face. When he reached them, he nodded at Brandon and held his hand out to Cami.

"Ms. Carmichael, it's a pleasure."

"Thank you," she said politely, shaking his hand.

"This is my dad," Brand said.

"I could tell," she replied. "There's a definite resemblance."

Brand nodded. "Y'all hungry?"

"Yes. We haven't had dinner. I hope you've got something green. She likes tofu, hummus, wheat germ…"

After looking at Cami like she had a terminal illness, Brant said, "We can manage green salad."

"Stop it." Brant's eyes tracked Cami playfully slapping Brandon's arm. "Whatever you have is fine, I'm learning to appreciate the pleasures of poison."

"No doubt." Brant gave Brandon a reprimanding look about the affectionate familiarity the client's daughter was showing him.

Knowing what that look was about, Brandon just shrugged and smiled at his father. It was a silent challenge that said, "Some things are none of your business, old man."

"She's in Brigid's old room," Brant said.

"Okay. Meet you in the kitchen in a minute." Brandon tugged Cami in the direction of the sleeping quarters. When they reached the last door on the right, he said, "This is you. For the next few days."

That answered the question about whether or not he was staying. She wasn't going to beg or fall into a puddle. She was going to put a big girl smile on her face and let him go. After all, what other outcome could there have been? Since the moment she laid eyes on him, they'd been moving toward the day, hour, and minute when they would be permanently parted.

"It's not the Sherry Netherland, but you'll be safe."

She set her bag down on the bed. "And warm and dry."

She looked over at him in a way that asked if the past three days had meant anything to him. "And warm and dry." He repeated it quietly in a way that didn't reveal anything about his feelings. She was left with the impression that she could mean nothing to him or everything. "I'm going to my place tonight. After dinner. I've got stuff to catch up on. But I'll be back tomorrow and, if you need to talk to me, just ask anybody to get me on the phone."

Nodding, she wrapped her arms around her waist and walked toward where he stood in the doorway. "Okay."

"Let's get something to eat. I'm starved."

THE KITCHEN WAS standing room only as everybody wanted to hear the blow-by-blow account of what happened with the helicopter and the Dust Devils. People watched Brandon and Cami eat leftover Shepherd's Pie and salad while he told the tale.

Cami smiled at the whoops and hollers that went up when Brandon described shooting the gas tank.

He looked at her. "We felt the heat of the blast as we were hightailing it away. Didn't we? Just like in the movies."

She smiled. "Me more than you. Your back was being sheltered by *me*."

Everybody laughed at that and Cami was starting to feel less anxious about the strange surroundings.

"This big redheaded son of a bitch named Cannon Johns was wearing a Sons NOMAD patch. He's the one who drove us to that deathtrap you bought for us to fly home in. Said he's coming home after one more job."

"We'll be glad to get him back," Brant said. "And that plane wasn't a death trap. The former owner and I go way, way back. He would not let my kid get into a plane that wasn't safe. Just because something's old doesn't mean it's not serviceable."

"Feeling sensitive about your age, Prez?" said Rock.

"Fuck off," said Brant.

After dinner, Brand turned to his pop and said, "Where's Brash?"

"He's ironing out that deal with the McIlhaneys. Oh, and by the way, I didn't tell your mother anything about this, um, job."

Brand lifted an eyebrow. "So you're saying you want

me to keep quiet?"

Brant lowered his chin and scowled. "You know damn well that's what I'm saying."

"Sorry. But I'm not in the habit of keeping things from my mother." Brandon smiled in the most irritating way possible. "What's in it for me?"

"The first thing club members have to learn is how to keep their mouths shut."

"Yeah. So?"

"So what's in it for you is a patch." Brant couldn't help his grin when he saw emotion move over Brandon's face. "Voted you in today." Brant slapped him on the shoulder with a big paw and rocked him back and forth a little. "Tomorrow's Friday. We'll have a pig roast tomorrow night to celebrate. Everybody'll be here."

Brand swallowed hard. He hadn't realized exactly how much he wanted that until it was in his grip. "That's…"

It was just as well that Rescue interrupted him because he wasn't sure what he was going to say.

"She like dogs?" Rescue said and Brandon deduced that he was talking about Cami.

"I don't know." He started to ask why, but then realized where the question was coming from. "Let's find out."

"Cam?" She was talking to one of the wives, but turned to Brand's voice. "Do you like dogs?"

Confusion registered on her face. "Of course. What kind of person doesn't like dogs?"

"A bad sort," Rescue confirmed with complete conviction.

"The reason he's asking is because one of the club's interests is in canine security. Rescue trains dogs to take care of people. If it would be okay to leave one of the dogs with you tonight, it would be an extra measure of security."

The idea was instantly appealing.

"If you're sure the dog won't suddenly decide that I'm the bad sort of person in the middle of the night."

Rescue looked a little horrified and a little offended. "My dogs are stable, missy."

When she realized that she'd inadvertently insulted Rescue, her eyes flew to Brand for help.

"I'm sorry, I…"

"Don't worry about it. Rescue's dogs *are* stable. He's the one we're not sure about."

Rescue grumbled. "I'll go get Daisy."

Brandon turned back to Cami. "I'll stay until you're settled in."

"You're coming back tomorrow?" She licked her bottom lip and looked around, which he'd learned she always did when she was nervous.

"Count on it." They sat on the side of the bed in the room Cami would occupy. "And I've got a present for you."

"What?"

He had her full attention.

"A new will. Airtight. Leaves everything to your parents in the event of your death. I'm going to send it over tomorrow morning. You'll sign two originals in the presence of witnesses and a notary. One of those originals is going to the club's safety deposit box. The other is going to be personally flown to Boston by a reliable courier of our choosing and filed with probate court. Then that courier will deliver a copy of the will and proof that it's been filed with probate to Trey Michaels. In person. By tomorrow afternoon, he'll have no reason to want you dead."

Her eyes filled with liquid. "Why didn't we think of that?"

"I don't know." He reached over and swiped a tear trail away with his thumb. "Maybe because you were scared. Your dad, too."

She nodded. "Thank you."

"It's almost over. Meanwhile, you see those windows?"

She looked up. There were windows across the north wall, but they were up high at ceiling height, and were only six inches high. They let light in during the day, but no one could see in from outside, not even from a great distance, and certainly no one could get in.

"Yes."

"They were designed to protect people we care about. You're safe here."

She wanted to ask if she was a person he cared about, but Rescue arrived at the doorway.

"Daisy says she's ready," Rescue affirmed.

Cami looked in the direction of the doorway and instantly fell in love. Daisy wasn't just a dog. She was without a doubt the most beautiful German Shepherd in the world. Cami was sure of it.

Daisy was a black and tan Shepherd with eyes that said she was smarter than most people and a doggy smile that could have been an arrogant smirk.

Rescue led Daisy over to Cami. He reached out and patted Cami on the thigh. When he did, Daisy put her nose to Cami's jeans-covered thigh, sniffed for a few seconds and then sat down. Rescue unfastened the leash attached to Daisy's collar and handed it to Cami.

"She won't let anything happen to you," Rescue said.

"Will she let me pet her?"

"'Course. She's affectionate. She'll snuggle up in the bed with you if you let her."

Cami reached out to pet Daisy and Daisy responded by pushing her head into Cami's hand. When she laughed, Daisy's ears came up as she studied Cami, apparently liking the sound of the woman's delight. Brandon agreed. It was nice.

"You ever had a dog before?" Rescue asked.

"No. But I wanted to. I'm keeping her."

"You mean forever?" Rescue asked.

"Yes. I mean forever."

He chuckled. "You're gonna owe the club a chunk of change. She'll go for about fifty thousand."

"Done."

"Not up to me. I just do the training. Brant makes the

deals. You'll have to talk to him."

Brandon leaned over and said close enough to her ear that she could feel his warm breath. "Don't worry. If you want that dog, she's yours."

"Oh yeah?"

"Yeah. I know the owner of the company. Really well."

To Rescue, she said, "I'll talk to Brant tomorrow and ask him about terms."

"Up to you. Daisy don't care who she belongs to as long as she's taken care of." Cami doubted that, but didn't respond. "If Brant decides you can have her, I'll school you up on how to take care of her."

"Alright."

Rescue walked out of the room.

"He's kind of a character," Brandon said.

"I see that."

"It's a story."

"It always is."

"Yep." He sighed. "I better take off." She grabbed his sleeve. "Cami, you're okay here. Promise."

"I know. It's just that…"

"Get some sleep. I'm going to catch up on stuff and I'll be back tomorrow."

She turned loose of his sleeve.

"Okay."

At the door he turned.

"Oh. Your stuff probably won't make it here until day after tomorrow. So make a list of what you need, clothes, bathroom stuff, whatever, and give it to Rita. She'll make sure it's taken care of. But if you want particular, you know, labels or whatever, you need to specify."

She reached up and ran her hand over her hair. "My hair."

"What about it?"

"I don't think I'll ever get over being shocked when I see myself in a reflective surface. I can't grow it out, but I'd like to change it to a color that's like my own."

Brand's face softened. "I've gotten to know you like that so it looks natural to me. But I can understand how you feel." He actually had really good reason to understand how she could feel like an alien in her own body. "We can get somebody to come take care of it."

"That would be good."

AFTER BRANDON LEFT, Cami pulled on a night shirt and climbed into bed. When she reached for the bedside lamp switch, she noticed Daisy was watching her expectantly.

She patted the bed and almost shrieked when the dog came sailing through the air, jumping over where she lay, to make a perfect landing on her other side. Daisy turned in a circle and then snuggled into the side of her hip.

"Well, you're not him," Cami said, "but I guess you'll do."

Daisy let out a noisy and contented sigh.

At some time during the night Cami roused. Either she'd heard a shout and a woman's loud laughter in her dream or someone nearby was having a boisterous time.

She reached out and stroked Daisy's fur, which had an inexplicable soothing effect. Since the dog seemed completely unconcerned, Cami rolled over and went back to sleep.

The next morning Cami woke to knocking on the door. She looked at the clock. It was after nine.

"Just a minute!"

Rescue was at the door. "That dog needs to go out. She's not a machine, you know."

"Oh, well." Cami felt a little embarrassed for not anticipating Daisy's needs. "She didn't come with an owner's manual, *you know*."

She instantly felt bad about copping an attitude with Rescue, but it was bad enough being awakened without a *rude* awakening.

When Daisy trotted over to him, he reached down and petted her, but his expression never changed.

"Leash." Rescue was nothing if not succinct.

Cami was looking around for the leash, but Daisy beat her to it. She took the leash in her teeth and dragged it to Rescue, who fastened it on her collar. Cami had to wonder what else the dog knew.

She shut the door behind them, brushed her teeth, washed her face and put on the only clean shirt she had. She might have been tempted to stay where she was, but her stomach had other ideas.

There was no one in sight when she stepped out into the hall. The bartender, Rita, appeared to be washing glasses. "Hey," she said.

"Hey," replied Cami. "I was wondering if I could get some, ah, toast or something?"

"Sure. Go help yourself."

"Okay."

Cami made her way past the office. The door was open and Brant was on the phone. She continued toward the kitchen and found it empty.

There was a selection of fresh fruit by the sink, which seemed promising, and two enormous boxes of varied donuts on the table, which looked more like roll of fat lying in wait than yummy goodness.

It was a large industrial kitchen, built to make food for a lot of people at once. That meant that there were a lot of places where loaves of bread could hide. After opening and closing more than a dozen stainless steel cupboards she found the bread stash. Four loaves of white. One loaf of whole wheat.

She grabbed the whole wheat and plopped two slices into the high-speed six-slice toaster. While she was waiting she located peach jam, a saucer, a knife, a glass and orange juice. She could have sat down at the long center island table to eat alone, but she grabbed her breakfast and carried it out to the bar.

Rita seemed like a decent sort and she might learn more about the strange lifestyle of bikers.

"Can I join you?"

Rita turned around and smiled. "Well, sure. I don't usually get company between breakfast and beer."

Cami claimed a place at the far end of the bar near

where Rita was working.

"Brand told me you may be wanting to get some stuff today since you had to shed your own things."

Cami nodded. "If it's not too much trouble."

Rita scoffed. "It's no trouble at all. Not like I'll do it myself. I'll hand it off to one of the prospects."

"Prospects?"

Rita looked at her strangely. "You are a virgin, huh? Prospects are guys who want to be club members some-day. First, they get a try out that lasts months, sometimes years. Their commitment and loyalty are tested. *Severely*."

"Sounds like sorority rush."

Rita laughed. "I don't think so, honey." Rita set down the towel she'd been using to dry glasses, squirted lotion onto her hands, and rubbed them together. "Now, while things are quiet," she said in a conspiratorial tone, "dish the dish on Brandon. What was it like to be with him nonstop for, what was it, three days?"

"Yeah. Three days. What do you mean?"

"Come on. I mean he's a really desirable guy and you're about to be an unmarried woman. So…"

Cami didn't want to out Brandon if he was keeping brooms company, but surely he couldn't hide his orienta-tion from people who were this close to him.

"Nothing like that." She shrugged. "Maybe he's, you know, not into women."

Rita gaped for a full five seconds before bursting into laughter. "That's a good one. The boy is the definition of player. I guess he decided to keep it purely professional with you. Good for him. Business first. His dad would be proud about that."

"Are you absolutely sure about this?"

"There is *no* doubt."

Cami chewed a couple of bites of toast. "Have you…?"

Rita shook her head. "Noooooooo. But he's brought girls to parties and interacted with them in ways that, like I said, leaves *no* doubt."

While Cami ate she mulled that over. Perhaps he had put a wall between them so that he could take care of business. That would make sense. But it also meant that Cami had a chance to get her wish and find out what Brandon's kiss was like before the adventure came to a close.

On the tail of that thought, Brandon walked through the door. He looked over and smiled at her on the way by, but didn't speak. She gathered up her plate, her glass, and the jam and followed him into the kitchen. The refrigerator was open and he was bent over, looking for something.

Thinking, *it's now or never,* Cami set the breakfast stuff down on the island, swiped her mouth with the napkin to be sure there were no stray crumbs and tapped Brandon on the shoulder. When he stood up and turned around, she launched herself at him, grabbing both sides of his face and pulling him down into a kiss that was as klutzy as it was sincere.

Just as she felt him pulling back from her, someone

grabbed a fistful of her hair and yanked backwards. And it hurt.

At the same time she was looking at the face of an apparently shocked and surprised Brandon... *was his hair that long yesterday?...* a redhead was continuing to yank on her hair.

"What the *fuck* do you think you're doing?" the red-head hissed in her ear.

Brigid had known when she married Brash that she needed to steel herself for a lifetime of running interference between him and the women who wanted to get their hands on him. Guys who walk into a room and draw the attention of every woman there aren't born every day.

"I'm..." Cami grabbed at the woman's grip on her hair. "Let go of me!"

Brigid let her go, but shoved her against the counter when she did.

The blow to Cami's hip took second place to the fire on her scalp. She reached up to rub her head. As the pain began to subside, she looked at the two people who were evidently waiting for an explanation. She thought she knew every one of Brand's expressions, but that was one she'd never seen. And the woman looked ready to kill her.

"Brandon..."

He held up his hand as if to stop her right there. He looked at the redhead and shook his head slightly. She rolled her eyes and then they both started chuckling.

"Listen, sweetheart," he said.

"What do you mean 'listen sweetheart'?"

She glanced at the woman, who said, "This isn't Brand. This is Brash. *My husband*. Who also happens to be Brand's brother?"

Cami's gaze jerked to Brash. Her lips parted as she studied him closer.

"Yeah," Brash said, "his *twin* brother. I guess he didn't tell you."

"No," she said. "He didn't tell me."

Brigid motioned toward Cami's hair. "Sorry about the..."

It was Cami's turn to hold up a hand. "That's okay. Let's just forget this happened."

"You want to go see him?" Brash asked.

"Go see him?"

"Yeah. He's at work."

"At work. I thought this was work."

"Nah. This isn't *his* work."

"I can leave?"

"Not by yourself. But you can leave with me. I'll grab a couple of the guys. You'll be safe as mother's milk."

"I heard you got here with the clothes on your back," Brigid put in.

Cami looked from Brigid down to the rumpled shirt she was wearing. "What gave it away?"

"It doesn't look bad, but... You and I are about the same size." To Brash she said, "Let's stop by the house so she can change clothes. I can loan her a few things until her stuff comes."

"That's very kind of you. Thank you. And, about what happened with your, um, husband, it wasn't very good. I promise."

"Now, hold on," Brash said. "It's not like I was trying!"

"You better quit while you're ahead, beautiful," Brigid told him. "It's fine with me that she thinks you're 'not very good'."

She winked at Cami and started toward the door.

Brash followed her saying, "I have a reputation to maintain, you know."

"The only reputation you need to be worried about is what I think of you," she countered.

Brash paused at the office door.

"We're taking the girl to see Brand."

"No."

"What do you mean no?"

"I mean no. She stays here."

"Come on. I'll have three guys with me. We won't be gone longer than an hour."

"Three guys?"

"Yeah."

"Who?"

"Eric. Rock. Crow."

"Eric, Rock, and Crow." Brant seemed to be considering that.

"If Brand can take care of her by himself for three days running all over the countryside, I think the three of us can keep her safe for an hour."

"Okay. An hour."

"Might take just a little longer. We're gonna stop by the house so Brigid can loan her some clothes and stuff."

"How much longer?"

"Hour and a half." It felt like he was a teen again bargaining for a later curfew.

"Call if *anything* happens."

"Yep."

"*Anything.*"

"Got it."

"Wait a minute!"

"What?"

"Brand was sending people over with some papers for her to sign. You can't leave until after."

Rita peeked in. "Bawdy says there are people at the gate that Brandon sent over?"

"That must be them," Brant said, getting up and coming around the desk.

AFTER CAMI SIGNED, Brant and Brash witnessed for the notary, who was also the delivery person.

"We're going to the office. You want us to take these?" Brash asked.

The young man was wearing a suit with no tie, but even without the tie, he looked *all* business. He handed one of the originals to Brash and said, "Take this one. I'm on the way to the airport with this one." He held up the one he was keeping. "Got a flight to Boston. Things to do.

People to see. News to deliver."

Brash took the document and nodded.

"Well, ladies, nothing's keeping us here. Let me grab the guys."

Brash, Brigid, Cami, and Rock got into Brigid's BMW that Brash had given her for her birthday. The other two followed behind in a nondescript SUV because guys riding with SSMC colors on their backs tended to get noticed and getting noticed was contrary to the goal.

They pulled into the garage at Brash's house and put the door down before getting out of the car. Inside, Cami commented on the view.

"It's beautiful here. I didn't know Texas could be so… hilly?"

"Yeah," Brash said. "That's why it's called the Hill Country. A lot of people think Texas is desert, tumbleweeds, horse-drawn wagons. They don't ever seem to see the pictures of pine forests, beaches…"

"Alright. Alright." Brigid laughed. To Cami she said, "Don't get him started. Come upstairs and get some clothes."

A HALF HOUR later, Cami left feeling pretty in a red silk shirtwaist dress that stopped three inches above the knee. Brigid's shoe size was larger so she had to wear her combat boots.

"Oh, well," she said, looking in the mirror. "It's a look."

Brigid chuckled. "Goes with your hair."

Cami reached for her hair. "I can't wait to change it."

"One thing at a time," Brigid said.

She packed the things Cami was borrowing into a Gucci bag and handed it to her.

"This is really wonderful of you."

Brigid shook her head. "Purely selfish. Brash will participate in the profit from this job."

As THEY DROVE away, Cami commented on the house next door.

"Beautiful houses," she said.

"Believe it or not my in-laws live in that house." Cami looked at her. "Yes. Right next door. It's a good thing I like them."

"It is."

"Brandon owns the lot right there." Brash pointed toward a piece of grass with a few trees. "He's going to build a house someday."

"Huh." That was the most non-committal thing Cami could think of to say.

SHE SUPPOSED THEY weren't exactly inconspicuous as they entered the lobby of the modern high rise office building. As they got on the elevator she was thinking, "Four bikers, a redhead, and a spikey-haired blonde in a red silk dress and combat boots walked into a bar…"

On the other hand, Trey would be looking for a sophisticated woman with long mahogany hair, no bikers, no combat boots. It could be a brilliant version of hiding in plain sight.

Brandon had bought a downtown building on Congress between 6th and 7th before he moved the main offices to Austin. He took the top three floors and rebranded the building with the Germane name and emblem and was instantly admitted to Austin society and invited to join the exclusive clubs.

Cami didn't notice the building name and it wouldn't have registered as out of the ordinary if she had.

The six visitors stood facing the doors as the elevator rose higher. Cami was feeling some butterflies in her stomach. She didn't know if she was nervous about calling Brandon on his sexuality or if she was afraid of finding out that the attraction was hers alone.

When the elevator stopped, it opened directly into the reception area of Germane Enterprises. Cami was familiar with the name, which didn't really say much. Most people were familiar with the name and the sultry voice that delivered the TV ads.

"We don't always put our name on the things we make, but we're everywhere you look. We're the future. We're Germane."

The stunning brunette at the reception desk gave Brash a big Hollywood smile, while ignoring Brigid and Cami altogether. *Ugh.*

"He here?" Brash asked.

"Yes. He is." She started to open an intercom line, but Brash stopped her. "Not this time. It's a surprise."

Her smile fell. "But sir…"

"I take responsibility." To the three tagalong bikers he said, "Wait here."

Like good soldiers, they unquestioningly took seats on plush chairs.

Brash led the way to Brandon's office, the big one at the end of the hall that faced south and east. Cami stopped dead when she saw the name on the door.

Brandon St. Germaine.

No wonder he'd seemed familiar. She'd seen his photo at society events in Town & Country a hundred times. She hadn't pegged him because, who would have ever guessed that the CEO of Germane Enterprises would show up at a New Jersey warehouse, impersonating a bodyguard. On one hand, it explained a lot. On the other, it posed a maelstrom of confusion and questions.

Brandon appeared to be talking to air while wearing a Bluetooth earpiece that resembled a scifi implant. Gone was the four days of beard scruff he'd accumulated on the road. He was groomed to perfection, downright dapper in a charcoal gray custom made Italian silk and gabardine suit with a crisp white shirt and pale yellow tie.

He'd been appreciating the view from his office while talking lease terms on a Channel warehouse when he swiveled around to see Brash, Brigid, and Cami standing just inside the threshold of his office door. Cami looked like she'd just seen someone hit by a car, which made his own stomach sink in reaction.

It looked like he wasn't going to be able to take time carefully crafting retractions and revisions supported with plausible explanations about how wacky fall-in-love road trips can be.

The two of them remained frozen in a stare for a few seconds.

She broke eye contact first, looking around the room. There was a framed copy of the magazine cover that featured Brandon, the same one that instigated the life-altering events that led him to a father and brother he hadn't known he had.

First Cami stomped around the desk, grabbed the Bluetooth gadget off Brandon's ear and tossed it to the other side of the room.

Brash picked it up and said, "He'll call you back."

Cami walked over, took the photo off the wall, placed it in front of Brandon on his desk and said, "This you, bodyguard?"

Brandon couldn't stand the hurt he saw on her face. He swallowed so hard, his tie moved, before he said, "Yes. But I can explain, Rose."

"It's Cami! Don't bother getting up because I'm leaving. And don't bother reintroducing yourself because I'm not interested. There's not a single thing about you that's real. I don't know you. I don't know anything about you."

He hated the fact that he'd caused her more pain. Worse, he hated the fact that she hated him.

As she stormed toward the door, Brash looked at Brand, who said, "Thanks a lot."

"Hey. When you want me to keep secrets, you need to give me a heads up. She started my day with a big sloppy kiss that was meant for you. I brought her here so she could deliver to the right brother. If I'd known this would fuck things up, we wouldn't have come. You know that."

"She's supposed to be on lockdown until the threat has passed."

"She's safe with me. Got Rock, Crow, and Eric waiting out there in the lounge, probably flirting with your fake tits receptionist."

Brandon started toward the door, but Brash stopped him.

"Whoa. Whoa. Whoa. Hold on. You need to let her simmer down a little. Club's throwing you a party tonight. You'll have plenty of time to sweet talk the young lady into forgiving you for being you instead of the guy she thought she wanted." Brash grinned. "Take care of business. The girl's not going anywhere."

Brandon didn't look completely convinced that letting it go until later was the best course of action, but his brother deserved respect when it came to women. He'd managed to do the one thing Brand had never done. He'd created and was maintaining a long-term relationship with a woman that was giving all appearances of being of the *forever* variety.

"She doesn't like being referred to as 'girl'. She thinks it's demeaning."

Brash laughed. "Okay. It's official. You've got the bug. Welcome to the PW club. Don't worry about the hit to your balls. It's worth it. I wouldn't have picked you for somebody who looks so… rough and tumble."

"That's not… It's a disguise. But it still looks good on her."

He knew he sounded defensive, which made Brash's smirk grow even bigger. He didn't know how Brash could be having such a good time at his expense when he felt so damned miserable.

He tried to get his mind back on work, but if that happened, it was going to be the challenge of the day. Maybe the year.

WHEN BRASH WALKED into the reception area, Cami said, "Take me back," in an imperious way that had Brash raising an eyebrow at her.

"Yes, *ma'am*."

He emphasized the word 'ma'am' to make the point that he wasn't a lackey.

When they got back to the clubhouse, Cami went straight to the bar.

"Do you know how to make a Manhattan?" she asked Rita.

"Of course. I worked at the Yellow Rose before this."

"I don't know what that is."

"Never mind. Coming up."

Two minutes later Rita set a perfect Manhattan on the bar. Cami looked down at it. "You know the two cherries on top of the lemon twist kind of look like…"

Rita smirked. "Balls?"

Cami raised her eyes to Rita, then dropped both of the cherries in her mouth and made a show of crushing them between her teeth.

"Keep 'em coming."

"You sure? I made that stiff."

"Not the alcohol. The cherries." Rita smiled. "There's a nice tip in it for you."

"Yeah? I'll bet."

"No, really. Here it is. Free of charge. Don't spend another day hanging around lying liar bikers."

Rita laughed. "You know, being called liars? That's not the worst thing I've heard said about these boys."

Mimicking Rita, Cami said, "I'll bet."

Brigid sat down next to her. "Hey. Maybe you'd like a sandwich to go with that booze. Rita was just getting ready to make lunch, weren't you, hon?"

Rita shook her head no while saying, "Oh yeah. I was just on my way to the kitchen."

"Don't bully her," Cami told Brigid, who laughed.

"Nobody bullies Rita. If she *could* be bullied, she wouldn't have lasted half a day around here because every one of these men will try it at some time or another."

Cami turned back toward the bar. "Good for you. Don't take any crap."

Rita narrowed her eyes at Cami. "You're not used to drinkin', are you, sugar?"

"How much has she had?" Brigid asked.

"Half a Manhattan."

"I see." She half pulled Cami off the stool. "Come on. After you have something to eat you can have some more cocktail if that's what you want."

"You can keep the cock," Cami said. "I have no use for it."

"Well, alright then," Brigid said, "I will."

Rita laughed, but headed to the kitchen ahead of them and started pulling out stuff to make sandwiches for lunch. Over the next few hours, hungry guys would be wandering in and out. They might sit down and converse with whoever was around while taking a lunch hour. Or they might just grab a sandwich and a bag full of chips and take it with them.

Since it was a club party day, several of them were already hanging around the spit outside that was giving an entire hog a slow rotisserie smoking. Cami had noticed it on the way in, but had averted her gaze because the scene looked a little barbaric for her liking. It was pretty clear that everybody was in a good mood.

After they sat down at the table that doubled as an island and a counter height table big enough to seat twenty for a meal, Brigid turned to Cami.

"You know what the party's for?"

Cami looked blank. "What party?"

"Nobody told you? There's a big party here tonight. All the members and their women will be here. Brandon is being patched in."

Cami shook her head to indicate that she had no clue what that meant. "No idea."

"It means full membership in the club. He's going to get the SSMC colors you see the other guys wearing."

"The snake in the, ah, temple?"

"Yes. It's a very, very big deal for Brandon because his grandfather founded this club. His father is the president. And his brother," she smiled, "the one who's *mine*, is the enforcer. He grew up without even knowing he had a father or a brother."

"He told me that. How did that happen?"

"Their mother. She was like you. *Is* like you, I guess."

"Like me how?"

"Lots of New York money. Lots of family expectation."

Cami took a big breath and looked away. "Oh."

"I guess it's not that surprising that Brandon would fall for someone like you. I'll bet the two of you have a lot in common."

Cami thought back over all the times on the road when she'd felt inexplicably close to Brandon. She knew he couldn't have a similar background or history, but even as she kept telling herself that, he *felt* familiar.

"The way the story goes, she'd been a little wild and the behavior was becoming scandalous for the family. When she graduated from college, her dad brought her to Austin with him for the summer while he was overseeing development of the Yellow Rose."

"Rita mentioned that. What is it?"

"It's an exclusive golf resort designed to please even the most discriminating tastes."

"I hate to interrupt, 'cause this is a really good story and all, but I need to know what kind of sandwiches you two are having," Rita said. She pulled her hair into a ponytail, put on an Astros ball cap, and began washing her hands.

"You got some of that turkey cranberry salad from H.E.B.?" Brigid asked.

"No. They're out. I've got some Rita-made chicken salad."

"Celery?" Brigid asked.

"That mean you want it with celery or without?"

"Without."

"Then it's without celery." Rita smiled as she donned a clean white apron and made quick work of tying it in back.

Cami chuckled a little in spite of the fact that she was mad enough at Brandon to want to chew him in two.

"How 'bout you?" Rita asked Cami.

"I'll try that. You have wheat bread?"

"Yeah. We got wheat. Toasted?"

"Ooh. That sounds good."

"With lettuce and tomato?"

Cami looked at Rita like she loved her. "Lettuce and tomato. Without me even having to ask. You're my new hero."

"It was bad out there on the road, huh?" Cami was nodding and looking like she might cry. "Once you get away from the cities there's not much to eat unless it's been fried or put between two big white buns."

"Oh my God. You know!"

Rita laughed. "It's not exactly a secret, darlin'. I think everybody in the world knows that except maybe you."

Cami seemed to deflate a little at that observation. "You want that with fries?" Cami's eyes started to look a little wild, but Rita quickly put her at ease. "Just kidding. I'm not frying any potatoes today. Garland is having about six gallons of potato salad sent over from The Smokestack."

Brigid nodded in response. "I like their potato salad."

"Yeah. Everybody does."

"You were saying, about Brand's mother?"

"I don't know all the details. That's probably for the best. But Brant was the head mechanic at the Yellow Rose. They met when she got lost on the property and I guess there was a sort of instant connection.

"Long and short is that they fell in love. Garland got pregnant with the twins. Her father was insisting she go to Wharton. She couldn't say no to him. So she said no to Brant. Brant was so heartbroken she gave him Brash. His real name is Brannach, but he was always..." she smiled affectionately, "let's just say he doesn't hide anything or hold anything back."

"That's..." Cami looked spellbound and incredulous at the same time.

"I know. Heartrending."

Cami nodded. "So how did they, um...?"

"Get the family together?"

"Well," Brigid's eyes sparkled, "there's more."

As Rita put plates in front of them, she said, "With that family there's always 'more'."

"So tell me," Cami said.

"Brash was going to replenish his stash of peanuts at

the H.E.B."

"Peanuts? Brandon eats those like his life depends on it."

"I know," Brigid said. "They both do. So Brash was standing in line to check out at the grocery store and he sees a picture of himself on this magazine. The guy's in a suit and doesn't have long hair like Brash did, but you know, it was *him*.

"So he bought a copy of the magazine, found out who Brandon was and went to New York looking for him. When Brash turned up at Brand's office, the first thing Brash noticed – after Brandon's shocked look, was a big bowl of peanuts on his desk."

Brigid stopped to chuckle like she could imagine being there. "So the two of them figured out that the reason why neither parent had ever married, or even dated seriously, was because they were still in love.

"The boys decided they wanted to get to know the parent they'd never met incognito. Crazy as it sounds, they decided to switch places. They met somewhere in Colorado. Brash cut his hair to match Brandon's. Brand got tattoos to match Brash's and learned how to ride a bike. The way Brash tells it, he was a natural, like motorcycle riding is in the blood or something.

"You can imagine how complicated it was, but it worked. They were pulling it off without either parent knowing, but Garland had a health event so they had to come clean."

"What happened?"

"They were right. Brant and Garland had never stopped loving each other. It's kind of a happily ever after."

"It is." Cami nodded.

"But here's the real reason I told you all this. Brant and Brash both have heads for business. Like Brandon. But if you asked them about their identities, they'd say they were bikers who happen to be businessmen. Not businessmen who happen to be bikers."

She stopped and seemed to be waiting for a reaction from Cami.

Cami said, "This is good," to Rita, who waved a thank you over her shoulder.

"Point is," said Brigid, "Brandon felt like he had his father's and brother's affection, but not their respect. That's what this job was about."

Cami sat up a little straighter. "You mean me?"

"Yes. Getting you here safely was about earning their respect. Germane Enterprises might be in the top ten of Fortune 500, but that kind of notoriety only goes so far with bikers."

"Why are you telling me this?"

"I want you to see how much was at stake for Brandon. He couldn't let anything take priority over getting you here safely. Getting the job done."

Cami looked at Brigid like she was waiting for more. "This party is his reward."

"The respect that comes from earning the colors is his reward. The party is just an excuse to party."

"I heard that." Brant's gruff rumble rose over the kitchen noises.

"Well, it's true."

"Did you have a good outing?" he asked Cami.

She'd been bred to say, "Why, yes, thank you." But she was thinking that, maybe in that environment, in a space where Brash was accepted for saying what was on his mind, it might be the one time when she could tell the truth.

"No. I didn't," she said. "I discovered that your son is a lying sack of shit."

Brant stared at her for a few heartbeats before saying, "Tell me how you really feel."

How she really felt?

How she really felt?

How did she really feel?

Her eyes filled with liquid that threatened to spill over and soak the breast pockets of Brigid's pretty red silk dress that looked ridiculous with spikey blonde hair and combat boots.

She stood suddenly and rushed out of the room.

Brant sighed. "Yeah. That's what I thought."

He looked at Brigid who gave him a rueful smile and a shrug. "They'll either work it out or they won't."

"That the kind of philosophy they're teaching over at the University of Texas these days?"

Brigid laughed. "No, but maybe it's what they should be teaching."

Brant turned to Rita. "I'll have pastrami, heated up,

on that…"

"Rye," Rita supplied.

"Yeah, with that…"

"Brown mustard."

"Yeah. Got any potato salad?"

"Your wife is having truckloads of it delivered later. I got chips."

"Hmmm," he grumbled. "Give me Doritos."

"Okay." She grabbed three paper napkins and handed them to him with the bag. "Don't eat the Doritos and touch stuff without wiping off your hands. It leaves cheese residue everywhere."

"You're gettin' a mite bossy."

"Somebody's got to be responsible for keeping this place from turning into the pigsty it would be without somebody like me."

"I'm going back to my office and eat this. Then I'm going over to Wreck and Ride."

"I'm not your secretary," Rita said to the wall over the kitchen sink without turning around.

"Thank the Lord," Brant said, walking away with his lunch.

When he was gone, Brigid said to Rita, "What do you think of Cami Carmichael?"

Rita continued working without looking up. "I think she's perfect for him."

"Yeah," Brigid agreed. "Me, too. I better get back to my own bar. See you tonight."

"See you tonight."

CHAPTER THIRTEEN

C AMI WENT TO the door when she heard a knock. She didn't really want to go to the door with swollen eyes and a pink nose, but whoever it was knew she was inside. After all, where else would she be?

Feeling like there was no other choice, she opened the door.

It was Brigid holding out the bag with borrowed clothes and a few toiletries. "You forgot these."

"Thank you." She took the bag. "You've been really kind."

"Don't mention it. You know you've been through a lot of changes in a short amount of time. Then there was the whole thing with the helicopter. Emotions have got to be running high."

"I guess."

"Why don't you get a nap? Spend some time enjoying the feeling of being safe. Then get ready for the party tonight. You can have some fun. Maybe give Brand a chance to grovel?"

Cami was surprised that Brandon's sister-in-law would use the word grovel. Maybe she was the one who should grovel. She had to admit that she'd talked first and thought later when she was at Germane Enterprises. She'd also realized that Brandon had led her to believe he was homosexual because she was about to blow their chances at the last motel room available for miles, when they were both exhausted.

After shedding a few tears over feeling like she'd been blindsided, she gradually gained a little clarity and perspective on what had transpired. He *had* misled her about his sexuality, possibly for good reason, but he certainly wasn't under any obligation, moral or ethical, to tell her that he also ran Germane Enterprises, or to reveal his net worth. She had thought that not giving a last name was part of the client/provider wall that was supposed to have existed between the two of them.

She realized that she'd behaved badly at his office and regretted it. If she'd had a phone and his number, she might've even called to apologize. That was a lot of ifs.

She decided the best game plan was to put cold water on her face, go to the kitchen and get two slices of cucumber to put on her eyes and pull the puffiness away, take a nap like Brigid had suggested, then try to make herself look decent and wait for an opportunity to talk to him at the party.

AT FIVE THIRTY Cami was almost ready when she heard knocking.

Arnold's eyes automatically swept down and back up when she opened the door. Force of habit.

"Brant wants to see you in the office."

"Does this mean I've been summoned?"

Arnold raised his eyebrows. The concept of being cute about the president wasn't something that came up in his world. Ever. "Does that mean you're not coming?"

He was already trying to figure out how he was going to deliver that news to Brant and get away before being caught in the wave of reaction that would surely follow. Fortunately he didn't need a Plan B.

"No," she said as she stepped out into the hall and closed the door behind her.

Arnold gestured for her to go first.

She said, "No, you first. I insist."

He smirked because they both knew he was planning to walk behind and check out the shape and sway of her derriere.

"Whatever you say, Ms. Carmichael."

She followed Arnold to Brant's office.

He was on the phone when she arrived. He lowered the phone, but didn't end the call.

"Good news," Brant said. "Your ex is in possession of your new will and your father persuaded the judge to sign off on the divorce decree ahead of docket. Looks like you're shed of that son of a bitch. Officially. And your dad wants to talk to you."

He handed her the phone.

"Hello?"

"It's over. You're free. On the way to making him a memory."

"That's great, Dad."

"You don't sound as excited as I imagined you'd be."

"I am. Believe me. I'm just… A lot has happened. The makeover. The running. The…" her eyes went to Brant, who was watching her, "unusual company."

Brant's smirk said he wasn't offended and might even be proud of the description. She was thinking that bikers must take Smirk 101 when they're prospects because they were all pretty damn good at it.

"I'm sure it's been an experience, but it was worth it to be on the side of caution."

"Of course. I guess I'll be coming home tomorrow."

Brant looked away. He didn't know the girl, but he thought she didn't sound either happy *or* excited about the prospect of returning home and he wondered what had really happened out on the road with his older son, meaning the one who was older by thirteen minutes.

"I'll send the plane for you and I'll be there to pick you up."

"Thanks, Dad."

"Don't be nuts. You're my girl. Now put Mr. Fornight back on the phone."

She handed the phone back to Brant. "He wants to talk to you."

When Brant took the phone, Cami left the room to return to her temporary quarters. The clubhouse was starting to fill up with people who'd arrived for the party. Dozens of people she'd never seen before turned a curious look her way as she passed by on the way to her room. She didn't see a single person she knew, but the congregation of people who looked so different from what she was used to wouldn't keep her from finding Brandon later.

She was on a mission.

She might be headed back home tomorrow and never see Brandon again, but by all that was holy, she was going to get that kiss from the *right* brother before she left.

BRANDON HAD SPENT a lifetime developing the sort of discipline and single-minded focus it took to run a global concern. All gone in an instant at the hands of one medium-sized woman in a blood-red silk dress, bare legs, and combat boots, a sight that would possibly be burned into his memory forever because of the emotion attached.

He spent the rest of the day trying to free himself from the entanglements of tasks that had backed up while he'd been on the road. But he had to return to things again and again because he'd let his mind wander and that had resulted in questions down the line. Every decision he made was like a domino effect. He had to have his mind in the game. Not on the way red silk seemed to float around a beautiful body when the wearer stomped across a room.

At seven o'clock he was still trying to wade out of the maze of things that needed his attention, and was feeling conflicted. Germane Enterprises needed his attention, but so did the SSMC. After all, they were throwing the party for him in celebration of the greatest honor they could give. He couldn't be late.

On the other hand, bikers didn't run on a German train schedule. Flexibility was built in. If he didn't get there until nine, it would be no big deal. Still plenty of time to party. And plenty of time to find Camden Carmichael and make her listen to his perfectly reasonable explanations for making her sit on a toilet and look at his painfully erect Johnson while pretending to be gay.

He sighed deeply running through that scenario in his head. Try as he might, he couldn't find the words to get to the outcome he craved. He wasn't sure he could even form a coherent description of the outcome he craved. He just knew it involved a Cami who wasn't mad. Or hurt.

At nine he more or less said, "Fuck it," and walked out of the office. He used his key to take the private elevator up to the top floor, which had been redesigned as a penthouse when he'd bought the building. He changed into jeans, Ropers, and a black Henley. He'd found black was good for parties. No matter what rowdies spilled on you when they accidentally bumped into you, it never showed too badly.

At ten o'clock, Cami was tired of watching people eat, drink, and dance. And tired of watching the door for Brandon. Supposedly the party was for him, but it was looking like he was going to no show. She entertained the possibility that he'd rather not attend his own party than have to see her after the way she'd behaved.

In his office of all places.

She, of all people, should know that, to the head of a company, the office is sacred *no*-family-drama ground. Even knowing that, she'd made a scene.

Setting her red cup down on the bar, she made her way through the crowd seeking the solace of her room. A tall blond guy with light beard scruff grabbed her and twirled her into his arms when she tried to pass.

"Hey, darlin'," he said. "You can't be alone. If you are, it's my lucky night. If you're not, who's the stupid fucker who let you out of his sight?"

She opened her mouth to respond, but Brash was there before she could speak, shouting over the music. "She's not alone, Des. She's a friend of the club."

The guy named Des raised an eyebrow. "Friend of the club? That works for me. I want to be her friend."

He looked down at Cami and smiled with even teeth so white they could have been veneers. His lascivious grin might have sparked interest if she didn't already have strange, confused, and unresolved feelings for a body-guard who'd turned out to be a famous player mogul. *Christ.*

"She's not looking for new friends, Des. Brandon says so."

Des turned his attention to Brash. "Brandon?" After processing that, he burst into laughter. "He ain't here."

"He will be," Brash countered. "This is his party. Re-member?"

"Oh." Des's eyes slid to Cami. "She's for his party. Got it. Okay, sweetness. Some other time maybe."

Cami shot Brash a thankful look and continued toward her room.

Brandon had almost made it past the fire pit when Carlot spotted him.

"Brand's here! Man of the hour!"

Carlot gave him a hug and a few manly slaps on the back.

Within minutes the clubhouse had emptied, making Brand the center of attention. They all parted like the Red Sea for Brant, who came walking through the crowd carrying Brandon's cut. Anybody who saw the smile he was wearing had no doubt that the honoree got his own good looks from his father.

Brash was standing next to his brother when Brant held the leather vest up for Brandon to slide into.

Brand hadn't expected to feel emotional about getting his own cut, but it was a little overwhelming. He hadn't realized how much he wanted it until it was riding squarely on his back.

He accepted hugs from Brant and Brash, followed by the other club members who'd formed a line to offer congratulations.

From inside Cami's room, she had no idea that anything had changed because the volume of the music coming from the bar was the same. Rescue hadn't brought Daisy by because he wouldn't have expected that she'd go to bed early. So she was alone. She lay down on the bed and faced the wall. She wasn't ready to get undressed or take makeup off because there was a chance

Brandon might still come.

EDGE RECOGNIZED HIS chance. He slipped back inside, making sure that no one noticed. That wasn't a problem. Everybody was busy making a big deal out of the second heir apparent.

Like they said about the English princes. An heir and a spare.

When Edge's dad had sent him to Brant, he'd been delighted to find his way to the SSMC and thought he was going to live the life of a one percenter. But under Brant's leadership, the club was becoming a legitimate enterprise, a network of businesses run by people who just happened to ride bikes.

Hobbyists. The word sounded vile even inside Edge's brain. They'd become hobby riders and he'd never had the chance to pursue the life he was born for. Until Michaels had sent a guy to recruit him.

Edge was going to end up with as much money as the club made in a year, just for doing what he'd love to do for free.

The door wasn't locked. Bitch must be feeling right at home.

Cami didn't hear Edge come in. She'd dozed off and, even though the music was down the hall, it was still loud enough to block out ordinary sounds. Like footsteps.

She woke when the pillow was jerked out from under her head. The guy named Edge, the one who was just naturally repulsive, was bending over her, his face just inches from hers. He smelled like stale cigarettes and sour milk.

"Hey there, beauty. Your husband has a message for you. He says to tell you it's not about the money."

The lamp gave off enough light to see the look on his face and it told Cami all she needed to know. The guy was there to kill her.

He knew the moment she registered what was happening, and relished the fear in her eyes. It was a major turn on. And if he wasn't in a hurry, he'd have had some real fun with her.

When she tried to sit up, he moved fast, pressing her back down with the pillow over her face. At the same time he straddled her body to hold her in place.

Her muffled screams weren't heard by anybody but her. She fought to get free but the guy was stronger than he looked. Her legs were useless since he was sitting on them. She didn't even know if she'd managed to scratch him through his clothes, but her efforts hadn't resulted in any change in the pressure being applied to the pillow. Her nails had been cut short as part of her makeover.

When her lungs started burning because of lack of air, her body convulsed, trying desperately to find oxygen. Her useless screams were coupled with tears, but somehow, in the midst of that, she managed to regret that she was going to die without that kiss.

WHEN THE LAST of the guys had christened Brandon's new cut with slaps on the back, he looked around, again, for Cami.

As a few people had gravitated back inside, to the bar, Rita had returned to her station. When Brandon couldn't spot Cami outside, he went in.

"You seen Cami around?" he asked Rita.

She shook her head. "Nuh-uh. Might be in her room."

Brand headed down the hall. He knocked, but there was no answer. Realizing that she might not have heard because of the music, he opened the door.

Just in time.

Cami felt the sudden absence of Edge and the pillow simultaneously. He'd left his position, sitting on top of her, as quickly as if he'd been jerked away. When she first tried to inhale, nothing happened. Her lungs and throat seemed to have stopped working. But after several agonizing moments while her heartbeat thundered in her ears, she heard a sound accompanying air being quickly drawn over vocal cords.

That was followed by her body involuntarily squeezing air out and dragging it back in. After several repetitions her mind began to clear so that she could process something besides a desire to live. When she was breathing normally again, or close enough, she looked around.

Brandon had Edge on the floor next to the bed and was beating the man with his bare fists. Blood had splattered on his face, but neither that nor the look of rage detracted from his beauty. To her it made him even more the bigger-than-life guardian angel who kept her safe, who'd saved her from Trey Michaels at least twice. Maybe more that she didn't even know about, because he'd been smart, and dedicated, and resourceful, and committed.

She sat up and tried to speak.

"Brandon." Her voice sounded like a crow's whisper. "You're going to kill him."

Brand stopped long enough to look over at her. He'd been so outraged that the weasel on the floor under him would put his hands on Cami. He couldn't even get his brain to process that Edge wanted to kill her. But that was exactly what had happened.

Thank God...

He looked at her beautiful face. Her eyes were wide and haunted-looking, her mascara smeared around her eyes.

Dragging his gaze away, he pressed his fingers to Edge's throat. "Too late," he said simply.

There was no pulse. Brandon had pounded Edge with so much force, one of the blows had driven nose cartilage up into his brain. No doubt that was what had caused blood to spray all over his face and clothes.

"He's dead?" she whispered.

"Yeah," Brandon said, failing to give a shit. "But you're not."

At that moment he decided there was only one thing in the universe worth having.

It wasn't money.

It wasn't the respect of the SSMC.

It wasn't the thrill he got from riding a Harley Davidson on Bee Caves Road at three o'clock in the morning on a warm Austin night.

It was the woman staring at him like she felt the exact same goddamned way.

In one fluid movement Brandon tore off his brand new cut and the Henley under it, exposing the body Cami had once called godlike. Wordlessly, she welcomed him into the cradle of her body, encircling him with arms and legs as he lowered himself over her and gave her the kiss she somehow knew she'd been waiting for.

For all her life.

They were both aware that there was a corpse on the floor by the bed and that its blood was pressed between them, mingling with their own fluids, but neither one cared. Both were focused on making love as if their lives depended on it.

Brandon pulled Brigid's cashmere dress off Cami and threw it toward the foot of the bed. He'd been dying to touch her perfect tits since the night she'd put them on display, thinking he was 'one of the girls'. He licked her nipples through her lace bra. Part of him wanted to take his time and enjoy getting to know her body, but the dominant part was feeling frantic about needing to be inside her.

It was evident that she was feeling the same way because she was pulling at his belt buckle, trying to get his pants down. He got up on his knees, unbuckled, unzipped, and shoved his pants down in a hurry, allowing his erection to spring free and bounce enticingly.

She moaned in response.

Taking that as an invitation he ripped the little matching lace panties away from her body and shoved into her in an athletic thrust that made her cry out, to the extent possible with her hoarse voice. He knew she was dripping wet and didn't think he'd hurt her. So he kept going.

Hoping she understood that what was happening between them was, in his mind, a claiming fuck of epic magnitude. From that moment, regardless of courts or clerics or family or anything else under the sun, she was his.

And nothing was going to change that.

Ever.

Judging by the way she grabbed onto him and chanted his name, he was guessing she did understand.

He adjusted the tilt of her pelvis so that he was coming in contact with her clit every time he plunged in and out. Her reaction was nothing less than spectacular. He was vowing to remember that position so that he could experience what he was witnessing over and over and over.

When she came, he exploded and thought he might have actually seen stars, which he'd previously thought was a stupid trope in romantic comedies. It turned out that stars are possible, under the right circumstances.

A dead body.

And the woman you'd kill for.

When he collapsed he rolled them onto their sides. He was still in her, lying on top of one of her thighs.

"Jesus, Rose."

"It's Cami." After her breathing began to even out, she said, "You saved my life again."

The only response he could make to that was to pull her into another kiss, to remind himself that she was very much alive.

When he pulled back, he said quietly, "I killed Edge."

"I know."

"And I'm not sorry."

"Neither am I. Are you sorry about the other thing?"

"What other thing?"

"We just did it raw." He looked confused. "And I'm not on birth control?"

"You're not on birth control?"

"No. I didn't have any reason to be. I haven't been, um, sexually active for over a year."

"A year?" He sounded so incredulous that it made her feel a little embarrassed. She didn't know why. "A year," he repeated as if he was still trying to process that. She nodded slightly, looking away. Seeming to reach a conclusion, he said, "Your divorce is final."

"I know."

"That means you can marry *me*."

"Marry you? Brandon, we…"

"Love each other. Right?"

She searched his eyes. "Yes. We love each other."

VICTORIA DANANN

"I have the means to take care of a wife and child."

The entire situation was so absurd that she started giggling.

"Brandon, you killed that man. You've still got his blood on you."

He looked down. "Some of it's on you, too." He grinned.

She went on, "The body is right next to us. And you're talking about marriage and babies?"

"Yes. I'm glad to see you've been following along. By the way," he said as his penis went soft and slipped out, "that was…"

"Spectacular." The very word he'd used to describe it. "What are we going to do about…?"

"In a minute, when I feel like I can let go of you, we're going to get cleaned up and… Wait a minute. Why was Edge…?"

Brandon's mind began racing.

"I had drifted off, which is why I didn't hear him come in. That and the music, I guess. He said that Trey had sent a message for me."

"What?"

"That it isn't about the money."

Brandon rolled onto his back and clenched his teeth. "He bought off a member of the club. To kill you. Not even for money. Just to be a vindictive asshole of the most evil sort."

"Yeah. Pretty much."

He turned back toward her. "Like I said, we're going

to get cleaned up." He looked at his watch. "Then I'm going to get my dad and my brother in here and we're going to decide what to do. As a family. But tonight you're coming home with me."

"Okay."

They got in the shower and washed each other off between long slow kisses and the casual exploration of each other's bodies. Then towel dried.

Cami had found that one good thing about her closely cropped hair was that it dried almost instantly after a few passes of a towel.

"You can't put those clothes back on," she said.

"This used to be Brash's room. I'm betting there's something still in here."

He walked out and opened the closet. Sure enough. A couple of pairs of jeans hung there along with three of his brother's signature long-sleeve tees. He plucked the Rage Against the Machine shirt off a hanger and pulled it on.

When they were both clean and dressed, with slightly damp hair, but no mascara raccoon eyes and no blood, except for what remained on the front of Brandon's cut, he said, "You're coming with me. I'm not leaving you alone again tonight."

She nodded, liking the sound of that plan very much.

CHAPTER FOURTEEN

"WE'RE HAVING A party here, or hadn't you noticed?" Brant grumbled.

"It can't wait," Brandon replied, keeping his arm firmly around Cami.

Brash walked up. "You wanted to... Hey. That's my shirt."

"I'll get you a new one," Brandon said. "We need both of you in Cami's room." There was something about the look on Brandon's face when he added the word, "Now," that put his father and brother on alert.

Brant gave an almost imperceptible nod. Brash raised his eyebrows just enough to signal that he was on the same page.

"We probably don't want to form a parade," Brandon said. "We'll go on back. You come one at a time when you're sure nobody is paying attention."

Brant and Brash shared a glance and silent agreement.

Five minutes after Brandon and Cami had been back in the room, Brash knocked.

Cami looked at Brand.

"Let him in," he said.

She opened the door enough to be sure it was Brant or Brash. It was Brash. She opened the door wider, got hold on his shirt, pulled him in quickly and closed the door.

It took only seconds for Brash to survey the situation.

"Good heavenly Christ, Brandon. What happened here? Is that Edge? Good God Almighty. Is he dead? He's dead, isn't he?" Brash accused his brother.

"Yeah," Brandon said. "He's dead because he was trying to kill Cami."

Brash jerked his gaze to Cami who nodded solemnly.

All three of them turned at the sound of a knock on the door. Brash looked at his brother and the Carmichael girl then walked over and let Brant in.

"Alright, what's so...?" Brant took in the scene. "Good God Almighty, boy. Did that used to be Edge?" Brant's eyes went to Brandon's knuckles that bore the telltale signs of abuse. "What in heaven's name have you...?"

"Edge was trying to kill Cami," Brash said.

"He was working for her ex. Trey Michaels."

Brant gaped. "That's not possible. He's a member of this club. Been with us since he was a teenager."

Brandon, Cami, and Brash stared at Brant, who seemed to be having trouble processing the idea that one of the club members could betray them.

"Before he shoved a pillow over Cami's face he said he was working for Michaels."

"Jesus," Brant said, looking at the body then at Brandon. "Is that blood on your cut?"

"Yeah. It is. And I'm not cleaning it off."

Brant sighed. "Your grandad would no doubt approve of your idea of breaking in a cut."

"She's coming home with me," Brandon said.

"Is she now?" Brant asked, glancing at Cami.

"Yeah. She's not safe here." The challenge made Brant's hackles rise, but he couldn't argue with that when the girl they were supposed to be keeping safe had just come within a hair's breadth of the grim reaper. "Apparently the sick fuck she was married to wasn't only interested in her money. He wants her dead just because he can't stand to think about her living outside his control."

Cami looked at Brand like she was seeing him for the first time. She was astonished that he had that kind of insight into Trey's psychology, just from pieces he'd put together.

"If that's the case, you're gonna need more help than just clean up." He waved at the body. After glancing toward Cami, he turned back to Brand. "You think that apartment in the sky is easier to defend than this compound?"

"The best design in the world isn't worth a damn if the people are rotten."

Brandon had a point that felt like a razor in Brant's craw, but his kid was right.

"I know you're mad. You got every right to be. But

believe it or not, there are seventeen guys standing behind you who are just as offended by this breach as you are, even though they don't know about it yet. Maybe more so 'cause we've known him for longer.

"I can understand you feeling like it's not safe here. So take the woman and go to your place tonight. I'm gonna send four of the guys with you."

"Where are you going to find four guys who aren't drunk?" Brandon asked.

As much as Brant hated to admit it, the kid had a point. Again. They'd been getting sloppy, by club standards, in direct proportion to their conversion to law-abiding citizens. When this was over, Brant intended to give that some serious thought.

"You're right. How about this? Stay here tonight. You can take my suite. I haven't stayed in it for, well, not since I found out about you," he said to Brandon. "Your brother and I aren't drunk. We'll take turns sitting at that spot at the bar with a view to the door to my suite. If anybody comes near that door, we'll know it."

Brand looked at Cami. She nodded.

"Okay," he said. "What are we going to do about...?"

Brant waved him off. "I've still got some contacts from the wild and wooly days. We'll get it taken care of in the wee hours while everybody else is sleeping it off."

Brant pulled his keychain out of his pocket, took the key to the suite off and handed it to Brandon.

When Brand took it, he said, "I'm keeping her."

Brant nodded. "I figured."

Cami gathered up the bag she'd gotten from Brigid and her toiletries from the bathroom. With one last look at the body, she walked over and stood by the door, eager to leave.

"WOW. PRESIDENTIAL PRIVILEGE."

She was right. Brant's suite was more luxurious than she'd pictured, having seen the minimalistic approach to the design and decoration of the room she'd been in.

It was three times as big. With wide plank wood floors and a massive bed that looked like it had been carved by a Germanic family during a long snowed in winter. The only color in the room was brown, but it presented itself in so many variations of shade, texture, and material that it was inviting. Soothing and sexy at the same time.

"Soothing and sexy?" Brandon asked.

"Did I say that out loud?"

"Yeah. You did."

"I must be losing it."

"Understandable. Come here." She let the overnight bag fall from her hands, walked over and pressed her face into Brandon's chest. He put his arms around her. "You're safe."

"I feel safe right now. Right here. But I don't feel safe when I can't see you."

"You will. When I take care of this."

"How are you going to take care of this, Brandon? He's never going to stop."

"Oh, yeah." Brandon was nodding. "He is."

She pulled back to look at him. What she found when she searched his face was confidence and sincerity. He believed that Trey wasn't always going to be a threat.

"How?"

"All you need to know is that you're going to live your life free. Free of the past and him. Free of fear."

He could tell by the way she sighed that she wanted to believe him, but didn't. Couldn't.

"We haven't known each other a long time in minutes," he said, "but I think you know you can trust me, that if I say something is coming to pass, it is. Someday I hope your trust in that is as automatic as breathing in and out."

"I do trust you."

He smiled. "That was the soothing. Now for the sexy."

Brandon had been with a lot of women in his time and knew a lot about technique, but he found that making love was different from hooking up in so many ways. For one thing, he was constantly distracted by the overwhelming emotion. He finally gave up on technique and just allowed himself to *feel*.

They made love slowly. Thoroughly. And afterward, Cami fell into the deep sleep of exhaustion. Being a hair's breath away from murdered is depleting in every way it can be.

The walls and door of Brant's suite were thicker than the rest of the rooms, but Brandon could still hear the thump of bass from loud music and the occasional shriek or holler. Long after there were no sounds of music or voices, he lay awake, mind racing.

He pulled away from Cami, taking pains to not wake her, pulled on his clothes and shut the door quietly. Looking down the long hallway, sixty feet away, he saw that there was a pair of eyes identical to his own locked on his movement, just as his brother had promised there would be.

Brandon got a bottle of water out of one of the small refrigerators behind the bar. When he came around the bar, he noticed that Brant was asleep on one of the sofas.

He slid onto the stool next to Brash.

"I think I have a plan."

"Should I wake the old man?"

"I think so. Three heads are better than two."

"You think I could sleep with you two whispering like old women?" Brant said from across the room. He got up and walked to the bar.

"You want something?" Brash asked.

"Coffee."

Brash turned and started the pod machine. He knew how his pop liked his coffee. The three of them turned to see who was coming in at that hour.

Brant had set Bawdy on the gate for the night and told him to let the unmarked white van in. Quietly.

"These the people?" Bawdy asked Brant.

Brant nodded. "Stay on the gate." Bawdy turned and left like a good soldier without having to be told twice.

Brant was on the verge of deciding that the boy would make a good club member.

Brant showed the two guys to the room where the body was resting, in peace or not, and returned to the bar.

WHEN BRANDON FINISHED laying out the rough draft of a plan to make sure Cami was rid of Michaels, he said, "I don't expect you to help me other than pointing out holes and problems. If I miss something and end up in a snare, I want it to be just me."

Brant and Brash shared a look. Though they didn't change expressions, Brandon could see a silent conversation pass between them, the result of having lived together for the whole of Brash's life.

The three stopped talking as the cleanup guys walked through the bar area carrying a black body bag. Brash went over and opened the door then closed it once they were outside.

"Of course we're going to help," Brant said in his gruff troll voice. "The club hasn't always been squeaky clean, you know. There was a time when things happened behind closed doors. Under the table. In the shadows. This is one of those things."

As the three were contemplating all the ramifications of that philosophy, the door opened and the cleanup crew passed through with all sorts of cleanup paraphernalia, on their way to take care of the room and make sure that not even a crime scene investigation task force could find so much as a molecule of evidence. They knew how to scrub and keep their mouths shut. They also knew how to invoice accordingly.

Brandon insisted that he, and not the club, pay the bill, which began an entirely new discussion about how to transfer money without leaving a trail.

CHAPTER FIFTEEN

B RASH TOOK THE cup of coffee Brigid offered him and leaned against the gray granite counter in their kitchen.

"Brand thinks he's in love."

"I'm not surprised."

"No?"

She laughed. "No. Cami reminds me so much of your mother."

"Mom?"

She angled her head with a skeptical look. "You didn't notice? Really?"

"No. Maybe you're more observant." Looking down into his coffee cup with a wicked smile, he said, "Or maybe you're just plain wrong."

"You're still thinking that's going to happen someday, huh?"

"There's always hope. You know how you told me you used to cut your dad's hair?"

"Yes."

"I need you to get out the scissors and brush up your skills."

"Don't make me play twenty questions," she said, leaning on the opposite counter as she took a sip of steaming coffee.

"I need a trim and I want to look just like Brand."

"Okay. Why?"

"Better if you don't know."

She set her cup down. "Most of the time I like better. This time I think I want to know."

He shook his head. "Sorry, baby."

She sighed. "I don't like this."

He shrugged. "Comes with the wife gig."

"Not making me feel better, Brash."

"How's this for better?"

Grinning, he took two steps forward and pulled her into the kind of kiss that made her forget who and where she was.

Brigid's body went to mush in his embrace, as often happened when he turned amorous. When he broke the kiss, she said, "It's a good thing Cami didn't get the full treatment or I'd have to kill her."

He laughed softly as he nuzzled her neck, humming.

BRANDON PLACED A call to Henry Bartholomew, COO of Claymore Industries, a small Boston shipping company that was in the process of being acquired by Germane Enterprises, but news of that was still in the confidential stage, yet to be announced. No one had leaked it to the Wall Street Journal or any other source Michaels would be likely to use.

"Say, Henry," Brand said. "I'm thinking about doing some business with Trey Michaels. I'd like you to set up a meeting if you would. Have him come to the City Club for lunch. Since he's not a member, he'll be impressed by that. I'd like you to feel him out about the possibilities of selling his Greek line to Claymore. You think you can do that?"

Bartholemew was overjoyed that his boss-to-be was demonstrating so much confidence in him. It seemed to settle the question of whether or not he'd still have a job after the acquisition dust settled, and gave him hope for advancement opportunity at the same time.

He was careful to mask his elation and not appear *too* exuberant. There was sometimes a fine line between amiable cooperation and boot licking.

"Of course. I'm honored that you're entrusting me with the task."

"Do it soon. Tomorrow if possible and let me know the exact plans."

"Exact plans?"

"Such as when you're scheduled to meet."

"Oh. Alright."

"Thank you, Henry. I'll be in touch about the results of your meeting." Brandon ended the call.

BRANDON WAS STILL stiff from having spent twenty-six hours in a car. The fact that he'd traded off driving with Arnold had helped, but he'd also had to listen to Arnold's idea of conversation, which consisted almost entirely of talk about women, worldwide wrestling, or himself. They hadn't flown because Brandon wanted no record of the trip.

Arnold had procured a rental, using his alternate identity. They'd made a point of avoiding toll roads where they might be photographed and time stamped as they passed through.

He'd instructed the yacht captain to move the Silver Garland from her home at North Cove out to Montauk and leave the key in the usual hiding place.

Brandon and Arnold parked at the Montauk lot, grabbed their bags, pulled the hoods up on their hoodies and tied them so only their noses and eyes were visible. It was almost midnight. So nobody would be around but the night watchman, if they had one.

Eric had spent two hours calling around to marinas before he located one that wasn't equipped with cameras.

He'd told them, "Well, damn it, I wanted cameras, but since everything else you offer is so attractive, I guess I can do without." He then gave them the name of the Silver Garland captain and told them to expect him.

It was easy to spot the Silver Garland. A yacht like the one that belonged to Germane Enterprises was unusual in *any* marina. It was a super yacht, big enough to even have a 'garage' for smaller craft, like a sleek speedboat, and a small inflatable.

Brandon found the key taped to a starboard fender. He and Arnold would sleep on board until about six the next morning. They'd leave before sunrise and arrive in

Boston around ten. Good weather. Clear sailing.

When they stepped inside and turned on the lights, Arnold whistled. "I've never been on anything bigger than a ski boat, but I'm thinking most people don't have this experience."

Brandon nodded. "Yeah. You'd be right about that. You sleep in there. I'll make breakfast in the morning. We'll eat and then get underway."

Arnold looked amazed. "You know how to cook?"

"You don't? It's a basic life skill."

"No man. It's one of the best things about women. Right up there with willing pussy."

"So you don't know how to survive without a woman nearby?"

"I don't know how to survive without a drive through nearby."

Brandon was in dire need of a breather from Arnold. "Whatever. I'm going to bed."

BRASH HAD BEEN tutored on people in the office, what they looked like and their relationship to Brandon. He'd also learned about Brandon's habits, what he did on arrival, where he was likely to have lunch, etc etc etc.

He was amazed how easy it was to walk through the doors of Germane Enterprises and have the employees look up and smile.

"Good morning, Mr. St. Germaine."

"Good morning, Mr. St. Germaine."

He nodded and returned the, 'Good mornings', in

kind on his way to the office.

Apparently all he had to do was show up wearing Brand's face and his clothes and, sure enough, people would be fooled. Somehow it had seemed harder when he'd tried it in New York.

He and Brandon had decided that, to be on the safe side, he would order lunch in. They thought it best that he not interact with Brand's business associates because they could easily take him into unanticipated territory.

Brash kept an office at Hollywood Wreck and Ride and ran his network of small businesses from there, but he could just as easily perform those tasks from Brand's office. All he needed was his phone and laptop, which he'd brought in a backpack that functioned like one that cost a hundred dollars, but had probably cost a thousand dollars. Brandon had insisted that it be part of his 'ensemble' when they'd stood in his closet picking out what clothes Brash would wear while he was gone.

If anybody ever asked, at least two dozen people would swear that Brandon St. Germaine had been in the office every day, all day, all week long.

TREY MICHAELS' DRIVER let him out in front of the building that housed the City Club. The sidewalk was busy with people trying to get lunch and get back to their offices in less than an hour. As he paused for a break in pedestrian traffic so that he could navigate his way to the entrance, he was intercepted by a young clean cut man in a dark suit who bore a remarkable resemblance to a thirty-year-old Arnold Schwarzenegger, but was not as big. As the man stepped in front of him, blocking his way into the building, he said, "Mr. Michaels?" His bearing wasn't threatening. He wasn't wearing a smile, but his expression might be described as pleasant.

"Yes. What is it?" Michaels used a practiced tone to let the man know he was aggravated.

"Mr. Bartholemew had another meeting this morning and is running late. He sent a car," Arnold waved toward the limousine at the curb waiting with passenger door open, "and asked me to convey his request that you lunch with him on the yacht instead."

Michaels didn't hesitate long. "Oh, well, alright." He got into the backseat and fiddled with his tie as the Arnold lookalike smiled and closed the door behind him.

AT THE SAME time, Mr. Bartholemew received a call from someone identifying himself as Michaels' assistant, saying that he was extremely sorry but Mr. Michaels couldn't make it and would have to reschedule. Bartholemew thanked the caller, but was inexorably irritated.

When he called Brandon's office to deliver the news, he was transferred to his assistant, who'd been told to say that he was in tele-meetings all day, the one exception being Henry Bartholemew.

"Yes. Mr. St. Germaine is in. Just a moment."

"Yes?" Brash answered.

"It's Henry. Michaels cancelled. No reason. He didn't even do it in person. Had an assistant call to say he was busy and would reschedule."

"Well, I'm sorry you were put out, Henry," Brash said, trying to minimize his drawl, as New York ears were sometimes sensitive to regional dialect differences. "He must not be very interested in doing business with us."

"That's my take as well."

"Stay and have lunch anyway. Have them put your bill on my tab."

"I wouldn't think of it. Let me know if there's anything else I can do."

"Let's play golf the next time I'm in Boston." He chuckled then added, "In the summer."

"Definitely."

THE LIMOUSINE STOPPED at the sailing club. Arnold had made arrangements to park the speedboat for a short time. After a short walk down the pier, Arnold jumped into the boat and began untying knots.

"What is this?" Michaels said. "You said we were going to a yacht."

Michaels' eyes followed where Arnold pointed out the super yacht anchored about three hundred yards east. Arnold felt a little satisfaction when he saw Michaels' eyes widen a little. A guy like him was hard to impress, but Brandon had managed to do exactly that. He stepped down into the boat and looked around, deciding where to sit.

"Sit there," Arnold instructed. "I'll try to go slow enough so that there's no spray."

Michaels nodded.

The 'garage' had been left open so that they were able to pull right in, under the yacht. When the boat came to a stop, Arnold began tying it off at the toe rail.

Michaels looked like he was about to get up.

"Hold on. Don't get up yet. Let me help you. Sometimes we get a sudden wake."

Without analyzing that statement for sense, Michaels stayed seated.

"Okay. Now you can get up."

Michaels rose and turned to make the step up to the walkway, but Brandon was waiting for him. He took pleasure in watching the progression of dawning realization that paraded across Michaels' face.

First there was confusion.

Then recognition.

Then realization that Brandon St. Germaine was tied to Sanctuary Security.

Arnold grabbed Michaels from behind and pinned his arms to his sides.

Brandon smiled. "Cami has a message for you. It's not about the money." He forced a washcloth that had been soaked in trichloromethane over Michaels' nose and mouth so that he had no choice but to breathe in.

The supply had come from Brand's dad. A small bottle. Brant had said that they could have easily made their own out of common household items, but that he'd gotten it from a friend of the club in order to avoid incriminating chemical traces around the club or at one of their homes.

Michaels struggled for less than ten seconds before he was out cold.

Brandon drew up the anchor by automated pulley and turned the yacht back toward New York. Halfway between Nantucket and Montauk, Arnold pushed Michaels off the end of the boat, weighted down with four eleven-pound barbell plates.

He closed the 'garage' door and found Brandon at the helm.

"He's sleeping with the fishes old school, boss," Arnold said. "They're gonna be well-dressed fish. 'Cause the clothes I was wearing are getting a salt water rinse. Just like you said."

Brandon smiled. "You did good, Arnold. The club won't forget."

"Yeah. I know. The club's been good to me."

THE SILVER GARLAND received permission to dock at Montauk at dusk. Brandon cooked dinner on board. They ate with the TV on. At dark, they locked up, replaced the key on the fender and started the long drive home.

Brandon called the captain while Arnold took the first shift driving.

"Pick her up at Montauk and bring her back to North Cove. I let some college buddies take it out fishing. They said they made a mess in the speedboat. So hire somebody to give it a deep clean. You know I don't like fish or fishy residue. So tell them to sterilize that boat. I don't want a single germ or fish blood molecule left behind."

"Yes, sir. I'll see to it tomorrow."

"Very good."

Brandon dropped the phone into the drink console, leaned back and closed his eyes. It felt like he'd spent far too much time in moving vehicles the past week.

He went to the penthouse first, threw all the clothes he'd taken into a hot water wash, showered, changed, and drove to the club. On the way he called Brash.

"You can go back to being you."

"Thank Christ. Where are you?"

"Ten minutes away from the club."

"Does Pop know you're back?"

"No, but he knows I'm supposed to be back tonight."

"That girl of yours has been antsy."

Brandon perked up at that. "What do you mean?"

"She's smart enough to guess what you've been doing. She's also smart enough to never name it out loud. But she's been nervous. Brigid and I took her to dinner. I thought getting her away from the club would help take her mind off things."

"Did it?"

"I think the only cure is seeing you back here. She's got it as bad as you."

Brandon unconsciously stepped on the gas a little harder. He couldn't wait to see her.

He walked through the clubhouse doors to a hail of greetings, but he was looking around for a spikey-haired blonde.

"She's in Brant's room," Rita said without being asked.

He looked down the hall. The door was closed and he couldn't get there fast enough. If it wasn't for the fact that he'd never live it down, he might have jogged down the hallway.

Cami answered the door.

Brandon was standing there looking uncertain. She'd changed her hair back to its natural mahogany color. She also looked at home in her own clothes that fit her perfectly and seemed to fit her personality. It seemed her bags had finally arrived.

"Brandon?" She was just as uncertain. She never wanted to find herself kissing the wrong twin again. Ever.

He rushed forward grinning, pulled her into his arms as he shut the door with his foot and ran a big hand over her head.

"I like it," he said.

She smiled, looking between his eyes and his delectable mouth. "And I like you. I missed you. A lot."

"How much?" he asked as he was backing her toward the bed.

"So much I don't want to ever be away from you again."

She felt a slight hesitation in his response, but ignored it because Brandon was clearly more interested in making love than talking. She was wearing a long nubby silk shirt over leggings and riding boots.

As he unbuttoned the shirt, he said, "Did I ever tell you what it did to me to have you show me your perfect tits in that see-through bra when we stayed at Flooded Bridge Motel?"

She grinned. "No," she said, as she reached for the button at the waistband of his jeans. "Did I ever tell you what it did to me to see every centimeter of your gorgeous lickable cock and believe that it was reserved for men only?"

As he pushed the shirt off her shoulders and let it drop to the ground he filled both hands with breasts that weren't overly large, but were satisfyingly heavy, like they had stick-to substance.

He raised his eyebrows and tsked. "Now you've done it." He unfastened her bra and pulled it away.

"What?" She lowered the zipper of his pants and plunged her hand inside, seeking the feel of velvety skin.

He drew in a sharp breath when her hand encircled his cock. "You said the word 'lickable'. You know what happens when you say that word?"

"Hmmm. Maybe. You want to tell me? After you take off those boots and those pants."

He shoved his pants to his knees, sat down on the end of the bed, pulled off his boots, then the pants followed. While he was doing that he watched Cami walk back to the door wearing just leggings and boots and turn the lock.

She returned to where he sat on the end of the bed, still wearing his midnight blue Henley, with a magnificent hard on pointing a perfect forty-five degree angle. He leaned back, supporting himself with hands flat on the bed, like he was proud of having made a mouthwatering erection.

She knelt between his legs. "You were saying?"

"I was saying that this is the most beautiful sight I've ever seen." He leaned onto his left hand, palmed himself in his right and gave it a stroke. Then he held it still. "Put your pretty pouty mouth right there."

She smiled. She didn't try to remove his hand. She encircled the head with her tongue, letting him hold himself, watching his reaction as she played with her nipples. His eyes were hooded, his lips parted like he was enraptured.

As she took more of him into her mouth, she reached down and played with his balls, alternating rolling and giving a gentle squeeze. She took her cues from his uneven breaths and the sounds he made as she learned what he liked, how he liked it.

He tapped her on the head. "Stop, baby. I want to come inside you."

She pulled away. "Playing with fire," she whispered. "Still not on birth control." But it didn't slow him down.

He grabbed the jeans that had been discarded and pulled a ribbon of condoms out of a pocket. "I'm pre-pared, but it's a temporary measure. You've already spoiled me for skin on skin."

He forced her to stand up, pulled her leggings down to her thighs and played with the curls between her legs while she drew in one gasp after another. Her hands went to his shoulders to steady herself so she wouldn't fall over.

He didn't think he could wait to get her boots and leggings off. So he turned her around and bent her forward until she caught herself when her palms hit the bed. Even in Brandon's feverish need, he was careful to be sure she was wet and ready for him.

The leggings were thick, tight and restraining, keeping her legs close together so that the extra squeeze created a delicious friction against her clit when he entered her from behind. For some reason, the fact that both of them were still wearing garments fed the urgency and heightened their arousal.

When Cami came, which didn't take long, she cried out loud enough that she would have been heard through the walls of any of the other rooms. Brand's climax followed seconds later as his thrusts became so powerful Cami had to fortify her brace to keep from falling over.

She'd never had a lover like Brandon. He was everything she'd ever wanted and more.

EVENTUALLY THEY SHED the rest of their clothes and lay on their sides facing each other in the dim light of one low wattage bedside lamp.

He knew what she was asking, wordlessly, her eyes searching his.

"You're free." His voice sounded gruff, even to him. He reached up and pushed her hair back even though it wasn't long enough to be in her face. "But it's not over."

Her brows drew together. "What do you mean?"

"You're going to have to leave. Start a new life."

She looked away, believing he was taking back what he'd said about them having a future together and not wanting him to see her distress.

"You'll get a job at one of the New York museums."

She shook her head. "Brandon, those jobs are plum. You don't just walk in and say, 'I believe I'll start work here today'."

It was his turn to look at her like she was being naïve. "Come on. You know how it works. I'll offer to renovate a wing and mention that I know someone… I'll gradually start spending more time at the New York office, making the party rounds. As will you. We'll run into each other. Start dating. Get our pictures taken together. Announce our engagement in six months. No muss. No fuss. No suspicion."

She blinked her eyes rapidly and took a deep breath when she realized he was laying out a plan. She didn't like the idea of spending *any* time without him, but six months wasn't forever. And if it got them to forever…

"I'd like to live here," he said. "I could give it up, but I just discovered my pop and my brother."

"That's okay with me. I want you to be happy."

"I want you to be happy."

"I am happy when I'm with you. I'm not going to like six months away. I like twenty-four seven."

He pulled her closer so that her face was nestled into

his neck. "Me too. But we can do this. It's smart."

"Brandon."

"Yes."

"Thank you for taking care of me."

"I discovered that it's my purpose. The most important thing in the world."

She sighed happily and snuggled in closer.

AFTER A WEEK Trey Michaels was officially declared missing. He had a lunch meeting with Henry Bartholemew on his calendar, but Bartholemew confirmed that he never showed up. Without a body, or a person with motive, or a family who cared about the victim, the police were not especially enthusiastic about dedicating valuable resources to solving the mystery.

For all they knew, Michaels had tired of his billionaire lifestyle and decided to disappear to Lichtenstein. Or wherever.

Cami stayed busy. She spent her days working at the Frick. She'd taken a sublease on the upper east side near the park, gotten in touch with a few friends from school who lived in New York, and made plans so that she'd be seen about town. But to her it was all part of the momentum carrying her forward to the day when she'd be with Brandon all the time.

As he'd said they would, they met at a party given by someone who'd become a mutual friend, and started dating. Brandon spent more time in New York than in Austin. Brandon and Cami finally decided to have a small wedding at the home of Cami's parents. That, however, was followed by big receptions in Boston, New York, and Austin.

Brandon gave Cami the lot on the bluff overlooking the river in Austin as a wedding present and told her she could build any house she wanted, but make sure it had a lot of room for kids.

As Brigid had suspected, Brandon's mother was crazy about Cami. She joined the campaign to suggest that grandchildren would be welcomed in the very near future. In the meantime, Cami's new favorite thing was weekend rides with the SSMC and their women.

SOMETIMES WHEN CAMI found herself alone, still, and quiet, her thoughts wandered to the two lives that were forfeit for hers. When that happened, she felt neither sadness nor guilt. What she felt was gratitude that she'd been lucky in love. She'd found a man who loved her enough to kill for her and never look back.

~

Sons of Sanctuary #3, NOMAD *March 2017*

Cannon Johns was a man who'd once had the world in his hands and lost everything. When he rode his Harley underneath the motel office overhang just after midnight, he was soaking wet and looking for the only comfort life still had to offer. The escape of sleep.

After being told there was no food available at that time of night, he pulled his ride into the room he'd just rented and went looking for dinner in the vending machines. When he was eight feet away, he saw movement by the Mountain Dew column. In addition to being bone weary, world weary, and out of options, he was out of sorts with no patience for shenanigans.

"Come on out of there and state your business." He had to raise his voice to a near-shout to be heard over the pounding rain.

After a slight hesitation, a small figure emerged in a yellow plastic poncho, the kind you can get at the grocery store for a couple of bucks. As soon as she reached up to pull the hood back from her head he knew it was a woman by the delicate size of her hands and the way she moved.

The light was dim, but he saw her clearly as if it was noon on a bright sunny day. His late wife had once told him that he had to change out the light fixture in the kitchen because "nobody looks good in fluorescent light". The girl standing in front of him was proof it just ain't so.

Her eyes were violet blue. And wide. He wasn't sure if that was because of fear or misery. Like him, she was soaking wet. Unlike him, she was shivering. Whether that was from fear or cold he couldn't guess.

"What the hell you doing out here, girl?" He looked around. "Something got you spooked?"

She licked her bottom lip. "No, ah, I'm just a little down on luck is all. I don't want any trouble."

"Don't want no trouble, huh?"

It wasn't a question. He said it as if it was a provable fact. She shook her head to both punctuate his assessment and agree with it.

"Yeah. Me, neither. At least not tonight."

ALSO BY VICTORIA DANANN

THE KNIGHTS OF BLACK SWAN

Knights of Black Swan 1, My Familiar Stranger

Knights of Black Swan 2, The Witch's Dream

Knights of Black Swan 3, A Summoner's Tale

Knights of Black Swan 4, Moonlight

Knights of Black Swan 5, Gathering Storm

Knights of Black Swan 6, A Tale of Two Kingdoms

Knights of Black Swan 7, Solomon's Sieve

An Order of the Black Swan Novel Prince of Demons

Knights of Black Swan 8, Vampire Hunter

Knights of Black Swan 9, Journey Man

BLACK SWAN, NEXT GENERATION

KBS, Next Generation 1. FALCON: Resistance

KBS, Next Generation 2. JAX: Repentance

KBS, Next Generation 3. BATISTE: Reliance

THE HYBRIDS

Exiled 1. CARNAL

Exiled 2. CRAVE

Exiled 3, CHARMING

THE WEREWOLVES

New Scotia Pack 1, Shield Wolf: Liulf

New Scotia Pack 2, Wolf Lover: Konochur

New Scotia Pack 3, Fire Wolf: Cinaed

THE WITCHES OF WIMBERLEY

Witches of Wimberley 1; Willem

CONTEMPORARY ROMANCE

Sons of Sanctuary MC, Book 1 Two Princes

Sons of Sanctuary MC, Book 2 The Biker's Brother

Sons of Sanctuary MC, Book 3 Nomad

YOUNG ADULT

R. Caine High School, Book 1 The Game Begins

R. Caine High School, Book 2 The Knight

R. Caine High School, Book 3 The Fool

Links to all Victoria's books can be found here…

www.VictoriaDanann.com

I sincerely hope you enjoyed reading *The Biker's Brother* and that you choose to continue the series with *NOMAD*.

Reviews are enormously helpful to me. Please take the time to follow a link back to the book you've just read and post your thoughts. A few words are often as powerful as many.

Victoria Danann

NEW YORK TIMES and
USA TODAY BESTSELLING AUTHOR

SUBSCRIBE TO MY PODCAST
Romance Between the Pages

www.romancecast.com

Victoria's Website

victoriadanann.com

Victoria's Facebook Page

facebook.com/victoriadanannbooks

Victoria's Facebook Fan Group

facebook.com/groups/772083312865721

Twitter

twitter.com/vdanann

Pinterest

pinterest.com/vdanann

Made in the USA
Middletown, DE
16 December 2018